The Cousins

PREMA RAGHUNATH

zubaan

ZUBAAN
an imprint of Kali for Women
128 B Shahpur Jat, 1st floor
NEW DELHI 110 049
Email: zubaan@gmail.com and zubaanwbooks@vsnl.net
Website: www.zubaanbooks.com

First published by Zubaan 2011

10 9 8 7 6 5 4 3 2 1

ISBN 978 81 89884 60 4

Zubaan is an independent feminist publishing house based in New Delhi with a strong academic and general list. It was set up as an imprint of India's first feminist publishing house, Kali for Women, and carries forward Kali's tradition of publishing world quality books to high editorial and production standards. *Zubaan* means tongue, voice, language, speech in Hindustani. Zubaan is a non-profit publisher, working in the areas of the humanities and social sciences, as well as in fiction, general non-fiction, and books for children and young adults under its Young Zubaan imprint.

Typeset by RECTO Graphics, New Delhi 110 096
Printed at De Unique, A 62, DSIDC Work Centre, Tilak Vihar, New Delhi 110 018

To,
the memory of Radha, Viswam and Jamby

Acknowledgments

A book like this couldn't have been written without the backing of several people over the years. Vital to this support was my childhood and girlhood, nomadic as it was, through all the various cultures in a nascent India, in which it was entirely possible to be both wholly Indian while retaining one's own identity.

There are also others who I must thank from the bottom of my heart—first and foremost, Urvashi Butalia, who saw in this book possibilities and agreed to publish a complete stranger's book. Thank you, Urvashi. Then my dear friends Sunita and Renuka who had such tremendous faith in my writing ability—what can I say, except thank you?

My aunt Chella Kailasam whose descriptions of an old and gracious Madurai made it all come, vivid and clear, before my eyes.

My sisters Sukey and Nimmi for being part of the background.

My children Satyaki and Durga (and their spouses) for understanding many things without being told and providing me with the peace and quiet in their London and New York homes for this book to be written.

And of course Raghu my dear friend of almost four decades, who has provided the backdrop that made this book possible.

1

Goutu

The place was an outback. Located as it was on the banks of a life-giving river, which cunningly took away lives as often as it changed its course. Let us leave it nameless.

But the year must be documented. It was 1921.

It is enough to say that this particular time, it was not the swollen river which was the murderess. Let us state that the real murderer had already been born three years ago in another part of the same presidency plotting, as he was at his mother's breast, his future murders.

This particular killing, though, was being done by fate, in the lying-in room, the smallest and darkest in the whole house. A slender woman gasped for breath. She did not draw the next one. Nor did the child she had just pushed out of her thin, emaciated body.

They were both dead. The midwife gave a quick, professional look at the genitals. A boy. Pity.

Somewhere outside was a young man, waiting with practised patience on the thinnai for news. Slim, dark with a weak, rather foxy appearance. The looks lied. He was not cunning but he was weak.

He looked back at the inner courtyard. The midwife was talking to his sister-in-law and his mother. His mother broke into loud wails. The young man recognized the sounds of death. He looked away as the whole house rushed in, caving in on him. His brother looked angry and his sister-in-law went back into the kitchen before the fires were made to die out.

She let her thoughts run on. She would have to look after the silly brother-in-law and the three surviving children now. The last one was just one year old. Her mother-in-law would play her emotional blackmail role. But the dead bodies would have to be disposed of first. Thank God the child had gone with the mother. She must not forget anything now, she must not lose her head.

In the resulting immediate chaos, people failed to notice several things. First that somebody went into the prasava-kattu and removed the dead girl's jewellery.

In the white cloth held out on the floor a quick change was made. The inventory was a natural one.

Thaali, diamond ear-rings and bangles. *Besari, bullakku and rettai-vaddai shangli. Golusu, metti.*

Second, her husband's trunk was opened and a property settlement deed mysteriously disappeared.

And third—and this was what lasted for the next eighty-odd years—no-one saw the one-year old Goutu crawling up to the back of the house and looking into the birth-death room. It was dark and a funny smell already hung in the room. Partly blood and mucous and amniotic fluid. Partly, just the dark.

Goutu yelled with fear.

She never liked the dark after that. She had to have lights. Even when she had forgotten her brief acquaintance with her mother, her death continued to haunt her.

Darkness was death. Light was life. She would remember that.

Narayani

'Don't cry, Goutu, please don't. I will give you this pavadai to wear.'

'I am not crying. Anyway not out of sorrow,' Goutu said. 'I am crying only because I am so angry.'

It was true. She never cried anything except tears of rage.

This cousin Narayani was one of the two she could talk to. The others all ganged up with their mother.

And Goutu learnt pretty early what she must do when cornered. She did not have too many feminine graces.

Goutu

I must never tell them, or let them know how scared I really am. If they know how weak I am, that old hag with her silk saris and her acid tongue will starve me to death. I have to fight, fight, for everything, the hand-me-downs, the hand-outs, the charity. These cousins of mine want me out, they want me dead. And I mustn't give in. The violin lessons, the master who likes me best, they mustn't stop. Will they stop? They might, if I am much quicker than the others and start playing varnams before they do, that silk hag will stop those lessons. I have to learn to pretend and I must tell more lies.

Right now, I am lying. You know, you'd be surprised if you knew how many lies I can tell. Do you know that everything about me is a big lie? I don't think anyone ever makes out when I tell the truth and when I'm lying! Sometimes, I myself can't be sure—there, that's a truth.

For instance, how many of you know that I'm actually meeting Subra on the sly? Does that come as a shock? I think I'll tell the truth for the next hour so that you know all about what is going on. Subra is charming, which my husband is not, and he has a sense of humour. He makes me laugh though the sex part is boring. Quite difficult to have to wait for my periods for sex, so that I don't get another baby. I have to wash the sheets myself, all that blood you know.

One thing I really like and that is a man who can be masterful. And another thing is speaking English. Yes, I like that. And Subra can speak English, yes my dear he can. You see, he served in the British Army and when the army was demobilized he came to live here with his sister. And I knew them. Who would have thought that boring old Kamala would have such an explosive looking brother? I didn't know that but I know how I look in that red silk sari!

So that was the downfall of both of us. His English, and my red silk sari. Now we meet every time we can which is nearly every day. More and more lies—those are quite easy to think up.

Enough my dear, I mustn't tell too much of the truth. Or that old silk hag, my aunt, will come at me with her stick and her diamond ear-rings shaking, shaking as if they will fall off. And my cousins, who all want me out of the house, because, truth to tell, I am the best looking, will help her to kill me. I mustn't die before I have had a chance to live life. Some people say I am a thayilla child, no mother, poor thing, they say.

One person who has caught my fancy in this hell hole is Krishnanand. He has told me that if I come to Madras, he will let me stay with him. Will he marry me then? Yes—I think that is what he means, otherwise how can a man and a woman stay together? Even if he is my cousin. Of course I can marry him, he is a cousin I can marry. Yes I think he wants to marry me. I will say yes to that, if my father ever comes and asks me, but he has to ask his brother-in-law first. Of course, my mama will say yes to this, he really likes me, his dead sister's daughter.

Krishnanand speaks English with a real accent. Phush, phush, and phush he says. Valli and Sivakami say that he is going to be sent to England to study. We will get married before that and I can go to England with him. Then my cousins will be sorry and the old silk hag will really sigh with envy. I'll kick them all and go.

Achyutan

The last bus was well on its way to Melur, carrying in its lurching interiors, the weak, dark young man with a sly, shifty look. Sitting by his side was a four-year-old boy, who had hurriedly been invested with a poonool so that he might give his mother and his day-old brother the right kind of send-off. Skinny arms had been shoved into a shirt several sizes too large for that thin frame and his legs showed under his veshti.

Why had Amma looked like that? Why had she become so white? Of course she was the most beautiful woman he had seen and he liked her fair skin, with its beads of perspiration when she had been working. The way her hair grew, low on her forehead. Lovely black hair too. He watched her plait it, funny, the way she did it. She would run the comb through her hair about five times, carefully open a bottle of coconut oil and rub it into her hair. The she would separate it into three strands and expertly bring over two strands and tuck them under her chin, and her hands, long-fingered and blue-veined, would take the three strands back and forth. She would be smiling at him and he was mesmerized by his own four-year-old feelings Then the ceremony of putting the flowers in, the famed malli of Madurai. She would then get up, the latest baby, now Goutu, on her hip and awkward with pregnancy, she would allow her diamonds to dazzle for a minute before she went off to light the lamp.

And why had she vomited blood a few months ago? They had not done anything about that. Only he knew.

But this mother, with her face all covered and funny and stiff, was not his mother. They said she had died. He glanced at his father. No expression. Should he ask him?

'Appa.'

'Enna pa?'

Another sidelong glance. No—he had better not. 'When will we reach Melur?'

'In another hour.'

'When will be go back to Pudukkottai?'

No answer. A vague unease gripped the boy. Snatches of conversation came back, adding to his dread.

'How can Narayanan have three children and bring them up?' someone had asked. Paavam Narayanan. He will leave his son with his wife's sister and go away with his two daughters. Perhaps he will leave them with his brother. No, he must wait for just the right amount of time, say six months, and marry again. After all poor Narayanan is only thirty-three. Who will cook for him? And young men who don't get looked after are apt to go astray. Yes, that is what he must do, without further delay. We know of the right people with daughters who would be glad to look after a young man with three children in return for some food and a roof over their heads and a thaali round their necks. What does it matter if they have to pay for all this with their bodies, after all that is part of the cooking.

For now, Achyutan looked away from his mind and concentrated on the winding ribbon in front of him. He was hungry and it was getting dark. The bus lurched forward and Narayanan rose, Achyutan followed. The tin box was lowered and two cloth bags followed. In one had been the last remains of the lady of golden arms, of the dark hair with the scented flowers. They had been lowered into the Vaigai, the river of the city that rose with the blessings of Meenakshi—and fell with the curses of Kannagi.

Funny how I felt on that day, thought Achyutan as he nursed his umpteenth drink, when I returned to the old house in Melur.

My father, the silly old man, was half in love with this sister-in-law of his. I can still remember the look, he thought wryly. And losing Amma like that, I felt a great pull of love for that old bitch, though I didn't know then that she was a bitch. I went in and there were my cousins looking scared and pious with all that vibuthi on their foreheads. Only Valli smiled, fat little Valli who grew even fatter with age. Nice girl, Valli. Odd guy she married, at fifteen, and produced I don't remember how many children. The other three were sitting there like statues.

The aunt took us in and there was some rice soaked in water in a corner of the kitchen. My mother only fed that to the buffaloes. I didn't realize then that for the next five years, I was to be no better than a buffalo.

'I had kept this for tomorrow,' she said, 'but now that you are here, you have it.' I was to learn that it was her way of giving anything, so that the receiver could feel the full burden of the sacrifice.

The buttermilk stank. She stood up and as she poured it from a height, droplets spattered all over the two of us.

My old man grunted with a half smile, which was his way of humouring her.

We finished that meal and rolled out the two pais. I got up next morning and heard my father say what I had known all along.

'I am going to leave him with you. Goutu and Dharma will be with my brother and his wife. My mother is there and she will look after the girls with Manni's help. Let him go to school with the boys. Let her things be here. I'll take them when I set up again.'

'Oh let them be here,' she mimicked. 'I am not going to eat them up.'

I didn't hear the rest.

There was a whine in his voice, I can recognize it now, and anger in hers. I hear it now, though I didn't then.

I must have another drink, right this minute. Those voices get to my head. You'd be surprised how often I hear those voices and you'll never guess who gave me the secret of Doing Away with Voices!

I'll tell you—it was Krishnanand. Who'd have guessed that that cousin of mine would grow up into such a dashing youth and have all the cousins at his feet? He went to England, you know, he said to study, but I don't think there was much study going on there. Though sexual exploits is also a kind of study, isn't it? If you count that as study, then Krishnanand has a doctorate. There was a story that wafted back to India, about his landlady's daughter....

Let me not get distracted. Yes, I will tell you about Krishnanand later, his story is not done. So that morning, my old man went back to Madurai.

She was angry all right. Whatever I did was wrong. In the thirteen days that it took for my mother to rejoin her manes, all her boxes had been brought here. They contained her vessels, it was right that they should go back to her father's house.

What else did they contain? I wish I knew. Because I never saw them again. The next five years... I really can't tell you about them. Funny things happened to my body, hair in funny places and some kind of a gooey substance coming from my penis, whenever I saw the girls at the bathing ghats. All this time, only Valli smiled and spoke. The others just moved away when they saw me.

To go back to Krishnanand. Yes he was exciting. Different. Totally non-judgmental, you know? You saw him at the funniest places. Just as you entered a shop to buy toothpaste. Or outside a move-house. And it would be the same. Marvellous jokes, harmless conversation and it always ended with 'How about a drink?'

God, was he different!

Of course his marriage to a top notch beauty failed miserably from the first day. But then, so did mine. We both should have stayed unmarried. He, because he was too interesting and I—I because I was too dull.

I suppose you could say my choice of wife was Freudian, she looked as I thought my mother had looked, though after all these years, I can't be sure. My mother's face has dissolved into the river of life. So has my wife's.

It's late, now, too late. The two girls, my sisters, just faded away. Dharma died.

And Goutu?

Goutu married a funny man. She fought like a wild cat with all those cousins on my old man's side till they finally got her married at sixteen to Mr Sobersides. He didn't like me.

He didn't like Krishnanand either, but that I didn't know until much later.

Dharma

Wonder why I feel so weak and ill. And I have a fever everyday which no-one knows about. Goutu is such a difficult girl that it must be making me ill just to take care of her.

I wish Amma hadn't died. When I grow up I want to become a doctor so that I can save lives. For that I have to study now. I must not tell anyone about this fever or I will be stopped from going to school.

My Periamma is actually quite nice. The other day she asked me why I was looking so thin.

'It must be your wonderful sister,' she said sarcastically. 'She is so friendly and obedient that it must be very easy for you to talk to her.'

Goutu is practising on her violin. But of course she hears. She sets the violin down and comes rushing out. 'Who would obey you?' she yells at my aunt's retreating back. 'Wait till I grow up. You will all be sorry you ever treated me like a servant maid!'

'Keep quiet, Goutu,' I say.

She turns on me. 'Why should I keep quiet?' she asks. 'I am not going to keep quiet. You can do so if you like. I'll fight and fight till I marry ...'

She stops.

A new fear enters my heart. Is she up to something with one of those silly boys who work for Periappa?

'Who, Goutu?' I ask. 'You have to tell me.'

'No I won't. You'll tell Periamma and that will be that,' she says defiantly.

I know that look. Once she gets that look, she will just get worse and worse till both of us start shouting.

'So don't tell me then,' I say trying a new trick. My insides are coloured red.

Goutu is surprised.

Actually she is quite green. Oh Shiva, why did I have to be in charge of this girl? Why isn't Achyutan here to help me with her?

She follows me into the room. The next look replaces the first one. Defiance has given way to puzzlement

'If you really want to know…' she begins.

'No I don't Goutu. It is all right. You keep it a secret.'

Goutu comes and sits on my bed. She is blubbering with excitement. 'You have to listen,' she says, 'you have to, have to, have to…' she chants.

'Seri, shollu,' I say, 'what is it?'

'It's Krishnanand.' Her voice has dropped to a rasp. 'We love each other. He wants to marry me.'

Krishnanand! I hadn't expected this. 'Did he tell you that?'

'No,' she says, looking like a firecracker ready to go off into a thousand colours, 'but he said if I went to Madras, I could stay with him. How can he and I stay together if we are not married? That is how I know.'

I look at Goutu's face and her slender body, just ready to burst into womanhood and a picture of my mother comes to my mind. I was five, Achyutan four and she just a year old when my mother died. Now she is twelve and I, sixteen. Achyutan is fifteen, almost a man.

We haven't met for over two years. Achyutan is in Madras, in a boarding school. Is he happy? Does he need anything? Want anything?

I think of Krishnanand, so much older than any of us, almost twenty now, and I can't say anything to Goutu. Krishnan's father is my mother's cousin and very, very rich. Goutu is a fool to think Krishnan will ever marry her. My rich uncle thinks my father is a weak wastrel who can't even get another woman to marry him, as he, my uncle, himself did when Krishnanand's mother died, in delivery.

Yes, Krishnan would have spoken glib words to this chit of a girl, who is so sensitive and spirited.

'Goutu,' I begin, searching in my mind for pink and pale blue words, words that don't mean much, for with Goutu, if you speak red words, she will make them purple with hidden meaning. 'Goutu, enna ma, you know how rich they are. They will go to some very rich houses for bride viewing...'

Goutu's face falls. 'Akka, he told me he would let me stay with him,' she says.

'He must have meant that you can stay with them, in their house,' I say, groping in the dark room for the handrail of common-sense.

But Goutu is not to be distracted. 'Krishnan meant that....'

She can't say the words. She leaves my room. I turn to the wall.

And I want to be a doctor.

Goutu

You know, dears, it was Dharmakka who tried to knock some sense into my head. But I was sure of Krishnan. The year was 1932.

Yes, I am very good with years, I think my daughters, who are all very clever, have got their memory for dates from me. Of course, my husband, their father, who has no sense of funny things or a joke or music or anything that grows or sings or dances with joy, is too clever for words. He it is who stops me from buying even half a rupee's worth of kadalai when I am pregnant with my last child. He is going to build a house, you see, with all that kadalai money! No but I have to stop telling too many lies and tell at least two truths a day so that I don't forget how to tell the truth altogether.

Yes, Dharmakka tried to tell me that Krishnanand, that man of the wonderful body and great looks, of laughter and fun and joy and chocolates and almost as many lies as myself, would marry a rich woman. But when he went to England, he wasn't married. He went for some big study, he didn't pass the exam. That I will grant my dull husband—he could pass any exam he chose to write and everybody would say Goutu how lucky you are, you have a genius for a husband. That is something he could do even till he was over eighty! My grandson, that beautiful boy who somehow my daughter and her husband managed to produce God knows how, went with him to buy shoes for the last course he took.

But now I want to tell you about Dharmakka, so enough about my grandson, even though he brought rainbows into my life.

She said that Krishnan will marry a very rich girl, one with a diamond necklace and diamond bangles. But where is Amma's jewellery, Akka?

Dharmakka looked down at her pale fingernails.

Her hands were very white and her wrists looked as if they would break. Her bangles would fall off and she would give them to me to wear. Dharmakka said she didn't know but I think she did. When so many diamond pieces appeared for Narayani's wedding, I think Akka understood where some of the diamonds had come from. So we did not have diamond necklaces and bangles and so I could not marry Krishnan.

We met before he left. He came to see grandfather and seek his blessings, he never really cared for blessings, he came to see me. There I was standing outside grandfather's room, looking through the crack in the door, drinking him in with my eyes and body, and he was standing, tall and handsome. He came out and caught my arm. I can feel it now, yes I think I can, I thought I would turn into lightning and illumine the skies. Actually not even Subra made me feel like that. The closest I can say I came to it is when I think of new lies and no-one can guess how I thought of them.

'Why are you going without me?' I asked.

'Wait for me,' he said. 'I will come back in three years and marry you.'

I would wait for a hundred years. So he kissed me, you think that in 1934 people didn't kiss? Where did all the people come from if their parents and others didn't know how to kiss?

He left the next morning. I was going to wait for him. Let them try and marry me off. I would run away. I would run away to England, I was sure I could manage that. I would love to see England, where all those white people spoke English.

But things didn't turn out quite like that. For one thing Dharma's wrists became thinner and her nails became paler till the truth was staring us in the face. Father came from Delhi, where he had gone to find work and took her away to a sanatorium.

Dharma

Goutu don't cry, I say as I leave. Yes, this little firebrand is sobbing and I don't want to leave her. But I have to go. My Periamma is afraid that her daughters will get this illness, or worse, no one will marry them. So go I must. Achyutan is here and I am surprised at the way he has grown and at his silences. Look after appa and Goutu, I say and he nods.

Goutu

After about six months, we see Pati sobbing and Periamma shouting. Many years have passed since the last time she has had to face this scene and now she is queening it over her mother-in-law. One fine morning Appa arrives with a little mud urn. It is what is left of Dharmakka and Achyutan, the ever-ready submerger of ashes, sends this too down the Viagai. Meenakshi and Kannagi are laughing their heads off at the city gates.

Dharmakka was right. Krishnan came back but he did not come to see me. His father's scornful answer to Appa's proposal was to show him some of the letters he had received from prospective fathers of brides.

And so it was that two years later, at sixteen, I married a grave, dark-skinned man who had no laughter, no jokes, no taste.

Actually he knew nothing about exciting things like lies and make-believe and a fancy, fecund imagination. He only knew about dull things like love and loyalty and truth. The funny fellow didn't even know how to turn me out of the house when I had that rollicking affair with Subra, with and without my red sari. I ran out of lies when he asked me about it, I had to agree that I had cheated. He told the girls too, the youngest only three or four and all of them scared. He asked me straight if I had slept with Subra—of course I had. Even the girls knew that.

He raved and ranted, his girlish voice going even higher with rage and disappointment. I wasn't sorry about anything. I'd do it again if I had the chance.

Subra and I said goodbye in style. I will tell you where and how later. I wasn't sorry to. It was getting a bit boring to listen to all that bragging, though it was like listening to a vellaikaran. And he didn't have a job, so I had to give him some of my jewellery.

Too many untruths, even I was running out of ideas. So out he went.

And I moved on.

Achyutan

What a huge fuss for nothing. This guy is all right, he is not so wonderful, why are the old man and Pati so keen on Goutu marrying him? Dharmakka wanted me to talk to Krishnan about Goutu, she would have done it herself, but she left, like Amma.

Achyutan had tried to, lots of times, between the tubes of toothpaste they bought or when suddenly coming upon him outside a movie house, they would walk in together and, having seen Charles Chaplin in mute action, or Stan and Olly doing the daftest things with not a muscle moving, walk out together again. Krishnan would be at his funniest best. Achyutan couldn't make up his mind about who was more side splitting, Krishnan or those clowns on screen.

Those were the times when Achyutan felt there was no-one quite like his cousin Krishnanand. Then they would go in, arm-in-arm, to some bar and have a drink. Only it was never just a drink. They would have three or four, with Krishnan becoming Kitchu and Achyutan becoming Atchu, and Kitchu and Atchu would be Laurel and Hardy. It was perfect, yes perfect.

Twice or thrice, before he metamorphosed into Atchu, Achyutan had tried to bring up the topic. But feebly.

'Aren't you going to get married?' or 'What kind of girl would you like?' or 'Have you met anyone special?' were his three attempts.

Krishnan would laugh uproariously. 'Who'd want a drunk like me?' was one standard answer. Why couldn't Achyutan say 'My sister would, like a shot!'

Or he would say 'I love women. I don't want to get tied down.'

So the moment had passed.

So here was the old man who had just got back from some remote village in the interior south, having found out about Seshadri and his family. Not very exciting. Staid, predictable, though Pati was thrilled. She thought his job wonderful, she said the predictions were that her granddaughter, who had been left in her charge fifteen years ago, was going to live like a queen. Seshadri did not drink or smoke. Narayanan had started doing both. His mother knew, and Goutu was getting on. At sixteen she could not be kept for another month in the house. Achyutan was unreliable, he too drank and his dearest cousin was that odavakarai Krishananand, her daughter-in-law's nephew. We don't know how long this can go on, said Pati. I may die any day and she will be left unmarried. So Narayanan must lose no time in making haste over the wedding preparations.

The passing of years and sublimation of desires had made Narayanan even quieter. His brother and sister-in-law—that is how he thought of her now, he had forgotten the word Manni—had cheated.

And so had the beautiful sister-in-law in Melur. When he went back to get his wife's chests, she feigned surprise and told him there was only one. The children, still with their vibhuthi, only older and bigger, were her witnesses. Achyutan, who had gone with his father, was speechless with rage and ill-concealed hate. 'Where are they, Chitti?' he had asked. (Her smile was the screen to her real feelings.) She was never one to betray emotion. Laughingly, she reminded him that he had been only four when her beloved sister had died and said a child could not be expected to accurately remember.

She has reneged, thought Narayanan. I should have listened to everyone and married again. I should have had my own home from the start. Then perhaps Dharma would be alive today. And the boy would have had his sisters.

There was nothing more to be said. The single chest was brought home, and his mother spoke about it to anyone who would listen, whether or not they knew Tamil.

Whatever it was, now he was going to see Goutu married and Seshadri would do fine.

Yes, I did almost speak to Kitchu about it but I never got to the point. Goutu's daughters are old now, married and Goutu is a grandmother.

What might have happened if I had asked? Would he have said yes? I don't know. For all our friendship, there was an unspoken barrier between us. I think it was a partition made of gold, behind which stood Krishnan, and he was too fun-loving to bring it up. And later I found out too much about him and the cousins.

But Goutu did marry the grave-looking Seshadri, who didn't have a single amusing thing to say and gave the impression of being the most boring companion on earth. What a wedding it was, with Goutu scowling and looking angry—not sad—and I on stage with her. The old man could not officiate because Amma was gone. So it was the uncle and his wife.

Goutu went off with her strange new family and within days she was at the frontier, with her new husband who worked there. Krishnan did not come to the wedding. I did not let him.

I thought it was all over between them. Goutu had children and her husband, the man of few words, went all over the country. Then why did I hear those strong trickles, and then a gush, of rumours that Goutu was having an affair with some man and Kitchu was helping her? Was he? I don't know.

I had lost touch with Kitchu. And Seshadri did not like me. Kitchu married his rich girl, studded with diamonds and rubies, but it was all over within the first three years.

Me, too. Though mine lasted longer. So where did all those children come from? I think I know the answer to that, though I can't remember it just now.

What was that mad desire, brought on by the dazzle of her ear-rings, the sweat on her upper lip as she worked, those blue-veined breasts, the plaiting of her hair, which I watched as a cat watches a mouse, ready to strike? Where had I seen that slow action, of the hair being divided into three strands, held in long slender fingers, brought expertly back and forth, secured under her chin? Why did I make a grab for her then?

Boy, bring me another drink. What money? Tell him I will give it to him tomorrow, okay, on the first.

Just bloody go.

Yes, so where was I? The mad desire that overtook me when those pink lips parted and I would fumble and enter and she would push me off. You smell of drink she'd say. You, my dear, are infinitely more intoxicating than any liquor I could ever get. When I see you like this, I think of another woman I used to know long, long ago and who I can't locate right now.

She'd smile, enigmatically I thought, but I wonder now whether it was just plain stupid, because she couldn't speak a word about anything interesting. A month later, she would be sitting as if some thunderbolt had fallen.

What's the matte?

I have missed my period. We are going to have a baby.

What, again?

It never ceased to amaze me that the result of sex could be a baby. I was always surprised.

I would watch her, plaiting her hair and she would stand up, awkward with pregnancy, with the latest baby on her hip, allow her diamonds to dazzle for a minute and then go out.

Hadn't I seen that somewhere once, didn't someone else also stand up like that and dazzle me with the beauty of her smile, not enigmatic. but clear and strong, with such love that I had felt a return pull of pure love? What had happened to that smiler, wait a minute let me clear my head of these fumes and I'm sure I can tell you if I concentrate.

She had been pregnant, too, and there had been a baby on her hip and some time later, she had gone. I think I did something to send her away, something with a lighted log and someone had held my hand to a lot of firewood. Who had been under that? The next day there was an urn, wasn't there, and the old man and I had gone to a place under a bridge and with someone yelling out meaningless words, I had put that urn into the waters.

Another drink please. What, no more credit! No, no please let me have a drink. I have to get to the bottom of this urn, it was made of red clay and I put it in the waters. Let me retrace my steps of that particular day.

Yes, most certainly there had been my old man and his elder brother and then we walked back to the house near the Meenakshi Temple. That house had belonged to my grandfather and I wonder what happened to it. There is a jumble of things coming up now. Various images, of smoke and bamboo sticks and strings and white cloth over a red sari, a white face peeping from out of it, Dharmakka crying as if her heart would break, Valli looking shocked, the aunts… no, that has gone. Was Krishnanand there? Perhaps. Or perhaps not. He had a way of never being there when he was needed.

I get it. The baby was Goutu and the pregnant woman who smiled at me with such love was—Amma? So I sent Amma to her death with that burning log of wood and made it final by putting that urn into the rushing waters of the Vaigai.

As D.H. Lawrence said, I had a chance with one of the lords of life and I have a sin to expiate.

Achyutan had always liked the written word and liked to think of himself as an intellectual. When he left school, the general consensus had been that Achyutan must join his father and be a son to him, whatever that meant. He would have to find out. Not that he wanted to. He had, by dint of adroit practice, learnt to pose as one who did not care. In Tamil it was called being 'don't-care master'. Achyut, in his assumed superiority, would affect that even that appellation did not bother him but secretly he was part hurt and part amused. So being a son to his old man might compensate for his wifeless state of many years. Poor Narayanan.

He was only fourteen when he finished matriculation and the thin boy with his stick-like arms and legs had grown into a young man with thin arms and legs. To his mortification, he had lots of pimples. When he had been with his Chitti, who he now referred to in his mind as that cow, he had not felt isolated in his ugliness. Her sons, his cousins, were both equally gauche. He thought of them as those dogs.

College in Delhi was nothing to Achyut, with his brilliant, if erratic, mind, although speaking was painful to him. Once he had got his degree, Achyut had joined a newspaper as the most junior sub-editor, and never had to speak. The speaking was done by other, more dexterous, employees.

Achyut's life in his mind and his conversations with himself were as rich-textured as his reality was impoverished. His vocabulary was as velvet, smooth and fine-finished, with the rarest hues shining out of its rich depths. His thoughts would race ahead, tumbling over each other, couched in such vital terms, with such colour that the resulting imagery, if it was made into paintings, might hang in some gallery, fascinating visitors and attracting artistic criticism. He spoke, in the land of his head and heart, in various shades of blue and green, red rubbing shoulders with purple and merging into orange and ochre.

None of these masterpieces ever saw the light of day.

His pale brown eyes, like the rest of him, were drab, almost lifeless. They would peer out from thick spectacles. He had long ago learnt to love his spectacles. They provided him with cover—no-one, especially the cow and the dogs, could possibly guess what he was thinking. That was good, for he thought a lot.

He learnt to cover up his inadequacies by speaking very little, and being very rude when he did speak. His father, being equally taciturn, had very little to say to him. Pati would burst into loud wails when he said something extra rude, oh why did she leave, she should have stayed, I should have been the one to be taken. This would disgust Achyut to the point of nausea and he would leave the house, with Goutu looking mutinous since she would not be allowed to go out.

And oh God, her violin-playing was infuriating. He thought he had left it behind because the cow's daughters were also being taught to play the violin, they would get good husbands if they played it well. Listening to the bow being drawn raspingly over the strings day after day had been like being thumb-screwed because neither of them had any idea of tone and tune. He had grudgingly got to admit that Goutu was better.

But the whole concept was flawed. One must play an instrument because, like his affair with words, it added to one's life. One must have a secret world into which one could retire, so that when the world became too much, there was that private place to get into. That private place could not, must not, admit anyone else.

The girls were all playing to ensnare husbands. Valli and Narayani had already gone off to be devoted wives, Sivakami was on the rack, so to speak, with a much older man who looked so worried and anxious that Achyut doubted that she would be fiddling all that much.

That left Goutu.

If he told her his Theory of Privacy, would she understand? But what would he say?

'Goutu, you don't have to play to please anyone. Music, art, beauty—these are for a person to enjoy.'

It was no use. She was a fighter and she would shout. Besides, there was that business with Krishnanand that Dharma had told him about. He knew his father had spoken to his uncle and his contemptuous dismissal with a brief refusal and his jibe about the dowry.

No. Krishnan would not work. He was engaging all the cousins in his little games. Achyutan had seen him with each of the girls in turn. He would make an appearance just before their wedding day and give them a little lesson in the sack. Those heavy-lidded eyes, that terrific physique, the deep-throated laugh—the smile—Krishnan reminded Achyut of an eagle, circling over the kill and swooping down, taking a bite, with the leavings remaining behind for their husbands, the crows.

In repose, Achyut thought, Krishnanand had that fine head, that hooked nose, the sombre, brooding quality of an eagle. Achyutan had seen it once or twice when the smiles gave way to seriousness, as he looked into his glass, stirring a drink, a quality that made Achyutan shiver. Krishnan's face never softened when he was reflecting, it hardened into the lines of a killer's face.

On these little pre-nuptial trips to Madurai or Madras or wherever the wedding was going to take place, the cousin in question would almost spring out of the door when Krishnan entered. In all that wedding chaos, it wasn't too difficult to draw attention away from oneself. Achyutan had seen it happening over and over again. There would be a slight rustle of the verandah door, Krishnan had positioned himself there straight after dinner. The cousin would come out, fly into his arms and there would be a triumphant laugh and quickly, quickly her half-sari would be abandoned and Krishnan's veshti would lie on the floor, a dull white under the dim light of an Indian sky. There would be some noises, movement and then, after all that wild excitement was over, there were tears. The sobbing would be punctuated by Krishnan's laugh.

But Krishnan was an accomplished seducer. No one was promised anything. Krishnan seemed never to forget the rich girls, one of whom he was being groomed eventually to husband. He was in no hurry, he would wait. He was being battened for better things. Not for him these little girls, with their innocence and naivète. Did they think one fuck made him their husband or did they think they were all his wives?

After one such adventure, Krishnan came to the startling realization that he had been well-named. Like the cowherd god, all the lasses of Vrindavan were his for the taking. He could screw up to one thousand women, maybe more, he had been created for that very purpose.

The next morning, it was all over. Krishnan would join the large crowd of boys who were eligible and being viewed as prospective husbands. The cousin who had only last night wept with joy and sorrow in his arms, could not even catch his eye.

He would just stay for the thaali-tying ceremony, as if making sure that the cousin in question was married and could not, ever, make life difficult for him. Then in a flurry of flowers and nadaswaram music, he would go off, to catch the bus that drove him back to freedom.

Had he fathered any children in all this activity? He did not know. Perhaps. The thought had entered his mind once or twice, because at least four of the girls had become mothers within ten months. But Krishnan knew that not one of them would ever give him away even if they thought the baby was his. They would kill themselves first.

But interesting to think that he could be a father without any responsibilities. Fun, too.

All those serious looking mamma's boys were congratulating themselves on their ability to sire children with just one night's action. All the time, they were stuck with second-hand goods.

Fun, what? Yes. Bloody good, clean, fun.

Achyut thought of Goutu. He must not be allowed to visit before the wedding.

Yes, he would be a son to his father.

Goutu

When Pati told me that the bride-viewing was successful, I thought I would die. How could father expect me to get married to this little man when I love Krishnanand? It was unthinkable.

So I did something that no one could dream of, I wrote him a letter and told him to come and take me away. How did I post the letter? Oh that was easy, I just had to think of something I must, at that very minute, tell the girl next door.

No, I did not get a reply. He cannot write back, someone might catch him at it. What he will do is to come here at the right time and take me away. But there is not all that much time left. Even the thaali has come and the ceremony of the diamond ear-rings is over.

My wedding sari is of a kathari-poo colour, the pale heliotrope of the naked-new brinjal flower. It has a red border and a three-finger gold border, I can just as easily get married to Krishnanand in it. No I don't mind the whole city, the world talking, anyway I will go away with Krishnanand and let Pati and Father face the music. Achyuta is here, Pati can complain to him.

Not two days are left now and no sign of Krishnanand. Tomorrow evening is the janavasam and the next morning it will all be over. I will be Mrs Seshadri. Goutami Seshadri.

He is here! I can almost feel him in my bones. There he is, god-like, those heavy-lidded eyes, the laugh.

Achyut is talking to him. Why can't my brother smile at his brother-in-law to be? What a sour face he has! What are they saying? Why is Krishnan going down the stairs and why is Achyut coming in and telling me to go back inside?

Things happened so fast then that I can't quite remember how Krishnanand was sent away, but sent away he was and I, hysterical with weeping, got married two mornings later and started life in some frontier town in the Himalayas with a man whom I did not know, did not love, did not want to sleep with. But then he wanted to sleep with me, that was his right and the nightly groanings and moanings would be replaced by silence and niggardliness. Though one thing I have to admit, he was very good at housework. He had been trained for it, his mother had a baby a year and he had all but helped her in childbirth! He could do housework with such precision and care, I don't think many men could copy him in that. It was all too strange. And stranger than anything was the first time I used the word Amma in my life. That was to his mother, I had to call her that. How funny it felt, that word, as it left my mouth, with no accompanying feeling. Just like that—Amma!

Do you think it funny that I haven't mentioned Krishnan after that nightmarish evening? He had got married to someone made of gold and rubies. I heard about it but did not go. Madras was too far away.

All the same, I knew that we hadn't said goodbye to each other. Ours was to be a never-ending affair. Even I could not have guessed at that time how never-ending it would seem.

Something that happened a few months later proved that we were meant for each other.

We had gone for a walk and let me tell you walking in the mountains isn't easy especially if you are pregnant, and I was pregnant then, and I saw at a distance a girl who was surely Tamil, with her silk sari and her diamond ear-rings. She was standing outside a shop.

My ordinary-looking husband, I was actually quite ashamed of his looks, was by my side. As we passed her, I smiled. She did not smile back.

She had the fair skin of aristocracy, she must be having a car, her father must be a rich man. So why is she standing here? I looked past her into the shop and even the baby in my womb lept with excitement!

For there he was, my god, in flesh and blood, that familiar back, the head on those fine shoulders, that black hair, combed back, those arms, those legs.

I did not care who saw me. I rushed into the shop.

'Krishna, Krishna.' I shouted.

He turned around. Why was the smile so fixed? Wasn't he happy to see me? Why didn't he come forward, leaping as I had done?

'Hello, Goutu,' he said. He looked out and his eyes were guarded. Guarded, too, was his face.

That quiet man, my husband, was smiling his shy, awkward smile. I couldn't believe I had married him. When there was this man on the planet, I had married this fellow with his oily hair, his pimple-scarred face, his sober, half-smile.

Krishnan and I came out, he careful not to touch me and I ready to hug him.

So this red-faced rakshasi was the ruby and diamond girl he had married. Her name was Sridevi. I knew that.

The rakshasi turned around and walked on, not acknowledging any of us. Krishnan followed.

I looked on, and this man by my side said 'Who was that? A friend of yours?'

A friend! No my dear husband, he is my lover. I love him, not you, never you.

Although I couldn't help thinking, as I looked at his plain face, that there was something different about his question, 'A friend of yours?'

So wasn't he going to rave and sulk? Act suspicious? Was I allowed to have old friends then? That too, men!

'No,' I said. Careful Goutu, think. This is a wonderful opportunity. Here is Krishnan and your husband, dull man, thinks he is your friend.

'He is my cousin,' I said.

'Oh', said my husband,' then we must have them to our house for tiffin. In my family, we always invite our cousins for tiffin if we meet for the first time after marriage.'

I looked at him again. He is ugly, then why did I feel something like respect for this man? What is the word for this behaviour? I have not ever seen anything like it. So I don't know the word.

As I lie down by his side that night, I think sharp, painfully happy thoughts of Krishnanand. My breasts are aching and the heart inside my breast is no different. It is a wild, turbulent sea, like the beach in Madras and Bombay. It is going this way and that. The baby inside me keeps pace.

Though one thing keeps coming back to me. Is he a friend? And, we must call them to tiffin.

What a silly thought to have when Krishnanand is somewhere on this mountain station, breathing the same air and walking the same streets.

I turn my back to him.

Is he a friend? Says my mind and, we must have them to tiffin.

Krishnanand

On the way home from the shop, Krishnanand walked very fast, ahead of his wife, showing her that he was in some way displeased.

He was scared, plain scared. For the first time in his life, he had run out of gambits.

His wife trailed behind, majestically, she did not seem to notice his displeasure or his speed.

He knew what was awaiting him at home. The icy looks, the wooden face, the disregard of his manly superiority.

She did not care for his looks, the ready laughter drew no answering laugh as it had done with all his cousins. She did not wait upon every move of his.

Not for her the sudden brushing of his arm, the sidelong glance of pure desire and adoration his cousins had favoured him with.

Sridevi, for that was her name, was the girl his father had always wanted for his son. It was his way of making it up to Krishnan for having given him a stepmother and a bunch of stepbrothers and sisters. Krishnan had looked down on all of them. He did not dislike them, they were too beneath him for such strong feelings, he was merely contemptuous. He, of the fair good looks, the fine figure inherited from his mother and her brothers, of the winning ways, did not have to dislike anybody.

As for him, he was only used to being adored.

He remembered the bride-viewing ceremony. Sridevi's father was one of the most successful doctors in Madras and Krishnan's father was flattered when he was approached by mutual friends for this formidable alliance. For that is what it was, a political alliance. The old man knew about his son and, although he had been too busy either siring children or being nasty to them, his fear was that Krishnan would spoil it by marrying one of his nieces.

They had driven up to Sridevi's house. His father had been nervous to the point of hysteria and all through the drive, had kept up a steady stream of instructions, punctuated by a blaring of the car's horn. Krishnanand recognized this to be his father's way of pleading with him.

'Don't say no,' his father was saying, actually using a civilized tone of voice, for the old man was known for irascibility. 'We are honoured...,' he could not speak any more, would not, in case the spirits of evil, known for their glee in mortals' misfortunes, overheard him, dropped whatever chaos they were creating in another's life and came rushing over to sabotage his life and that of his son.

Krishnan was curious. What was so unusual about this family that his father was being reduced to a quivering mass of anticipation and fear?

He soon found out.

The car drove up a long driveway, there was a palace at the end of the drive and the car came to a screeching halt.

Just a desultory servant on the huge, pillared verandah to welcome a prospective groom and his father and aunt! Unheard of! Usually the bride's father would be pacing the floor in breathless anticipation, with fruit and flowers and lights on full blaze, with a wife hovering round in the inner room, a glimpse of her grandeur showing in the rustle of her silks and the bangles tinkling against each other.

This was no ordinary father, though. He was a doctor, one of the first Indians in the presidency and had a practice which grew with each telling. No one quite knew what the extent of his fortunes was. He went to clubs and mixed freely with the whites. His wife played tennis with the white women, though in the regulation nine-yard sari. She also played cards. Did she, er, drink? No one dared to find out. Krishnanand found the thought of having a drink with his mother-in-law vaguely comforting. He wouldn't mind starting right now.

They were shown into the magnificent chandeliered drawing room. There were sofas, and carpets covered the floor. His father had a moment of pure panic. Should he remove his shoes or should he keep them on? He decided on the latter, wrongly as it turned out, because when the venerable doctor came out, bright and nonchalant, he looked pointedly at their shoes. Krishnan's father stuttered with embarrassment. 'I'll take my shoes off,' he said. 'So much more comfortable!'

Krishnan was more and more intrigued. Who was this man who could reduce his father's acid tongue to such sweetness? His mother's brother's wife, who had accompanied them, was less flustered. She lived in Bangalore, a cantonment town known for its cosmopolitan clubbing. The army had levelled the ground. Presently, her smile was the one she reserved for those she thought her equals.

Refreshments were brought out. The father, instead of jumping up and serving them himself, waved the servant in their direction. Nothing much on the plate to show that they were honoured guests, more as if they were part of a queue.

The aunt's special smile had become a trifle frosty and his father was looking tired with the effort of uttering niceties. Krishnan, with his newfound British graces, after all he had just returned from England where, though he had failed in all his qualifying exams, he had discovered P.G. Wodehouse and modelled himself on Bertram Wooster, thought it time to take matters into his own hands.

'Shall we go on with what we came here to do?' he asked, with his best laugh.

There was a shocked silence. Then everybody spoke all at once, the father sent for the mother, which meant the girl would also come out, and order was restored.

Sridevi came out and the effect was, simply put, dazzling.

She was covered with diamonds. Her sari, to this day Krishnan could not be sure of its colour, was scarcely visible. She looked directly at him, a bored expression on her face, she did not care whether he approved or not, it was the same to her and he knew this in a glance.

'Do you two want to talk?' the doctor was asking.

This did not happen even in Bangalore. The aunt had turned decidedly chill.

For once even Krishnan was dumbstruck. He just stared at her and his father was grinning.

After a few minutes of acute discomfort, someone suggested that they should go. Sridevi had gone in.

The doctor came up to the door. He had not held the car door open or asked what the verdict was.

'We'll let you know in a few days,' he said. The insult was intentional and the effrontery was breath-taking.

Back in the car, there was silence as they drove away. Krishnan felt more confused than he had ever done in his whole life. Who was this man who could hold societal norms in such disdain and yet have men like his father supplicating at his door? There was no answer to this. Except that, if one was rich, one could do anything.

They were home now. Krishnan's father looked at his second wife with some distaste. He felt it was her presence in his life that had got him this treatment. They all knew he had remarried and though they understood why he had done it, they laughed at him for it. And having so many children the second time round. ...Plebian. He ignored her frightened look.

'What did you think?' he asked with enforced geniality.

His brother-in-law's wife did not reply. She did not acknowledge the presence of this woman in her dead sister-in-law's place.

'Krishnan. I asked what you thought,' said his father.

'I thought them very rich,' said Krishnan lightly.

'Don't make a joke,' his father said shortly. 'We have to give them an answer in a day.'

'No Appa,' said Krishnan, 'he said he would call us.'

His father's humiliation was complete. 'He meant we should call,' he said. Then, with greater honesty, 'I would like you to marry this girl.'

Why? Krishnan wondered.

'All right,' he said. 'I will marry her.'

His father called on the doctor in his clinic and was met with a laugh.

'We are not yet sure if we want to send her so far away,' he said.

'My son has a very bright future ahead of him,' replied Krishnan's father, 'he is England-returned and.'

'But he did not get any qualifications there,' casually replied Sridevi's father, as he turned a paperweight around in his hand, as if it were Krishnanand who he was weighing up, 'there are a lot of England-returned doctors in the Madras area. They are all very keen on this alliance.' He looked at Krishnan's father directly and said, 'We shall perform the wedding as we had planned to do and she will get the jewellery she owns. We are not thinking of any money transactions if we agree to this match.'

Krishnanand's father thought fleetingly of his brother-in-law who he had turned away so scornfully with the confident assertion that his son was worth far more than he, Narayanan, could ever pay. He banished the thought.

'Oh, we have never thought of money,' he said with complete untruth, 'all we want is a good girl from a good family.'

The doctor's gaze was direct. 'I'll talk to my wife,' was all he would say.

And so it came about that in a month's time, Sridevi and Krishnan were united in marriage but nothing else. She did not show any emotion except when she left her father's house for Krishnan's decidedly more modest one. Sex with him, so exciting for all his cousins, those innocent girls he had bedded with so little feeling and so much vigour, was a duty which she might fulfil or might not. It was all her choice.

Her choice, too, when she would visit her father's home. The car would arrive and she would just inform them with no trace of emotion in her voice where she was going for the day. Krishnanand's father would just lower his paper and smile in a foolish, obsequious way. The stepmother and the brats were of no consequence. She would drive away and come back laden with parcels which she would take with her up to her room. No one dared ask her anything or ask to be shown what they contained.

Krishnan was by this time in a job in Delhi and so it was that, as part of his work, he was posted to the mountain town where Goutu and her husband lived.

Six months later, he sent for his wife and was informed that he must come and get her, she was not used to travelling alone. As he took her back with him, the two-day journey punctuated with the best packed food he had ever eaten, Krishnan learnt that she was a good match, as his father had said. A very good one. She treated him exactly as he had treated all his women so far. With boredom and unconcern.

Yes, it was a bloody good match.

Krishnanand had never been reflective but, of late, discontent was forcing him to think.

He did not like what he saw.

His wife operated on her own. She had her own money and she did with it what she pleased. Letters arrived and she read them and either tore them up or put them away in her bureau, part of her father's largesse, which could be locked.

'Why do you lock the bureau?' Krishnanand asked as soon as they had set up house.

She looked puzzled. 'Because I like to keep some things locked up,' she said, in the final way she had.

'Husbands are supposed to know everything about their wives,' he had said.

She was arranging some clothes in a shelf. She did not even stop what she was doing. Krishnan wanted to shake her, make her turn around, make her look at him. He did not know how to break through her indifference and assert his authority in the house.

'Why?' she asked.

He did not know why. But he could not allow this to go any further.

'Wives *have* to obey their husbands. That is their kadamai, their duty,' he said, his voice becoming loud, to make her understand. 'That is the way the girls in my family were brought up. They would never think of hiding anything from their husbands. They show all the letters they get, even those from their parents. They don't have money in the bureau which the husband does not know about.'

She turned around then. Her waxy features had turned a dull pink. Krishnan had learnt to recognize this was the signs of anger and he felt an answering spasm of impotent rage at his inability to control her.

'The girls in your family don't have money to keep in the bureau,' she said in her icy voice. 'Their parents are very scared they will come back home and so they write letters telling them to be good wives. I have money and I can go back any time I want to. My father is missing me and he would be very glad if I went home and lived in his house. And if you wanted a wife like that why did you not marry one of your cousins? I am sure they would have been happy to have you.'

She swept out of the room, calling 'Ramu!' He was their full-time help. Paid for by the doctor, of course.

Krishnan was speechless. Did she know? What, and how much, did she know? Had one of his cousins sent her a letter? Was that letter, at this very minute, burning a hole in the wretched bureau? The keys hung from Sridevi's waist in a ring which had an ornate face carved on it, of the goddess Lakshmi, her eyes and pottu embossed within rhinestones. Her grandmother presented each of the granddaughters with one such at their weddings. This was to ensure that Lakshmi, that most fickle of goddesses adorning the bosom of none other than Vishnu, would never leave the house of her granddaughter.

So how could he get the keys? Short of stealing them from her or hypnotising her, he could not manage this. And even if he did succeed, when would he open the bureau?

He could not sleep that night. The next morning, as he walked to his office, for the first time in his life, he felt his ineptitude. He *must* get those keys and he *must* get her out of the house so that he could ransack the bureau.

He must know who had written to her.

As he walked on, he saw Seshadri at a distance, cycling to work. He was wearing, as usual, white trousers and white shirt, his pant-bottoms rolled into small steel clips so that they would not flap and get dirty. That way he could wear the same pants for two days. His hair was combed back and even at this distance, Krishnanand could see it was glistening with oil, some of the oil mixed with sweat was making his dark face also shine. From the handle hung a cloth bag with the name of a shop written on it in Tamil. It must be his lunch, thought Krishnanand.

Krishnanand would not cycle to work. He thought it demeaning and he could not afford a car so he walked. Walking, according to Krishnanand, was more aristocratic than cycling, in England, people went for walks and they took their dogs with them.

Ah England! Krishnan stopped worrying about the bureau for the moment and his thoughts went back to England.

What a grand time he had had there! All that beer and those quaint pubs and the noise and those busty women! What beauties in their uniforms, and the excitement of Hitler and the way they talked! And they smoked too! The first time he saw a woman light up, his hand—with its beer mug—had stopped as if paralysed in mid-air, half-way to his mouth and he had stared.

'Wha' luv,' laughed the lady, 'never seen a woman smoke afore, then?' and the whole gaggle of women had laughed at his stricken face.

Not for long though. Soon, he was whipping out the matches with the best of them and lighting ladies' cigarettes and lighting up himself and they would all fall on him with merriment, because with old Hitler chucking it down, you never could tell, could you?

It was pure adrenalin, those air raid warnings, those sirens shrilling out the danger and everyone rushing down to the shelters and you could crouch on top of anyone till the danger had passed. You could hold just about anyone in your arms and kiss them and do all sorts of things and no-one knew or cared because this could be their last moment on earth. And in the final scramble to get out, one last lingering kiss and it was all over. You could climb back out into the road, the cold clear nights, with the black-outs, so clear that you could see the silvery moon, journeying across the sky, as she had been doing for countless centuries, in total disdain of mere mortals and their destruction, their loves, their lusts, their hates. And the stars! He had never known so many stars, but then of course he had never bothered looking up at the sky in his own country.

Seshadri disappeared and became a dot in the distance and Krishnanand was startled back into the present by the honk of a bus full of passengers.

The problem of the bureau had not been solved and Krishnanand reached his office. Boring, that is what it was. All these defeated-looking men with their silly clothes having to serve bosses who he knew had not even received an education in their own country, who, from his experience in England, he knew to be mediocre, drop-outs even, lording it over him and others like him in his own country! They had to stand up if the most junior officer came in if he was British. Yes Sir, Yes, Sir…! And those clipped British accents would tap out an order and they—he—must obey!

The bureau! It was now past noon and he could not stay. He must go home. He had to lie down and think this one out.

What did the Greeks, who had a name for everything tragic life had to offer, call it?

He thought the word was Nemesis.

Nemesis is what it was.

Now what do I do? I am walking home and that is not my home really. It is my father-in-law's home, an extension of the palace in Mylapore, Madras. The outhouse, would be more like it.

I don't really want to go back there, it means nothing to me.

Actually, nothing in life has meant much to me. My father is a spineless fool who married a rich and beautiful woman because his father was as manipulative as himself and loved money.

When my mother died, he went out and got married to a quiet scared little thing who I don't even know. Nor do I know the brats she produced.

So why was father so keen on my marriage? Why did he get insulted by Sridevi's father, why did he not say a thing? The same father, whose language to all his children is crude and degrading, was ready to do anything for this marriage.

Impossible to know why. Unless of course he felt guilty. What was that poster all over London? Give a home to a homeless waif.

That is a good description of me. I was a homeless waif after Mother's death. Going from uncle to aunt to cousins to step-mother. The uncles and aunts were paid very well and the cousins loved me for my body. The step-mother doesn't even know my name! Money and looks.

My father thought of me as a meal-ticket first and then, when he realized I wasn't going to be that, he wanted to make money out of my good looks and my stamp of foreign-returned.

But before I do anything else, I have got to get the keys of the offending object at the bottom of all this. The bureau. I have got to get the keys.

He was no nearer a solution when he reached home. Sridevi was nowhere to be seen, she had found some friends in an area a little way from here. The keys were with her.

He lay down and was awakened by a sharp hammering on the door. He rushed out and opened it.

To his dismay, it was Goutu and her half-baked husband. He steeled himself against Goutu's effusion and hoped his wife didn't return when she was going full steam ahead.

But his best cousinly manner did not fail him.

'Aha! look who we have here!' he said. 'At last you have thought of us, poor relations.'

Seshadri looked puzzled. Neither of the sentiments made any sense to his pragmatic mind.

'Oh what are you saying?' he asked, 'your house is furnished so well, how are you our poor relations? We are your poor relations,' he said decidedly.

Krishnan looked at Goutu, who for once was not jumping with scarcely repressed emotion. Pregnancy became her, he thought. It added a sheen to her golden complexion and her too-slender figure had gained in maturity. Her jet black hair snaked down her back in a single plait and the famed Madurai malli had been replaced with Himalayan roses. Pink, too, was her sari and blouse and she looked what she was—fresh, naïve, artless. Her smile hid nothing, it told him that she still found him sexually attractive and nothing had changed from that distant day when he had gone to ask for grandfather's blessings and she had been waiting at the door, and he had kissed her. She had said she would wait a hundred years for him. Did she remember, he wondered? Another glance, and he knew she did.

He went in to fetch what he could, maybe water? Damn his wife, she hid everything so well that a man could not find anything even in his own kitchen. He corrected himself, it wasn't his kitchen. It was his father-in-law's kitchen. One could not run a kitchen like this on a clerk's salary.

When he returned with the two tumblers of water, Seshadri was standing at the door, looking out.

'How much rent do you pay for this house?' he asked in his conversational, direct way.

Krishnan was nonplussed. Now everyone would know that his father-in-law paid for this house, his daughter could not live in a house even his servants might refuse.

'One hundred rupees,' he said. Actually it was two hundred.

'Oh,' said Seshadri, 'That is almost my whole month's salary.' He said it with so little rancour that it was impossible to mistake his enquiry.

Goutu was blushing with embarrassment. Money was never directly mentioned in her house. People either cheated or bribed or pretended they earned more than they did. 'Why do you bore others with these details?' she asked.

'He is a family member,' said Seshadri, 'he is like your brother. What is there if he knows?'

My brother! Goutu was speechless. Is that how he viewed Krishnan?

'Oh quite, quite,' said Krishnan, wishing to put an end to this conversation. Just then the garden door clicked open and Sridevi came in.

'Sridevi, see who is here,' began Krishnan, but Sridevi just nodded her head and went in.

He went in after her. He caught her by the arm, she winced with pain and he was glad he had reached her in some way. 'They have come to our house,' he hissed between clenched teeth, 'I absolutely order you to come out.'

She recognized the fury in his voice and decided to obey.

As soon as she came out, Goutu jumped up. 'I am so glad to meet you,' she said. 'I felt so bad that I couldn't attend your wedding.'

Sridevi smiled in her queenly way and Seshadri said, 'We have come to invite you to tiffin next Sunday.'

Sridevi looked at him. 'I never eat tiffin,' she said and took the tumblers in.

There was nothing more to be said. Krishnan said his goodbyes at the gate and asked for their address. He would come for tiffin the next Sunday, whether she did or not.

He stood there for a while, watching them go down the path, Goutu slower than usual and her husband following her.

As he walked back slowly to his front door, his mind was a whirl. This was how it felt to be married to a diamond girl. He felt like a cardboard cut-out. No life, no feelings, no reactions.

He then went in and took his pillow from the large bed they had, and without a word, went into the other room and shut the door. He didn't say a word. Nor did she. The next morning, it was as if nothing had happened. Ramu brought in his coffee and after a while he dressed and went to office.

The battle had come out into the open now.

Goutu

Well, that is how it all restarted. And none other than my husband was responsible for us meeting again. If he hadn't wanted him to come for tiffin, if Krishnan had refused, like that ill-mannered, arrogant wife of his did, if I hadn't invited him again, and if he hadn't come, none of this might have happened.

You may as well say then that the waves of the sea must not come and beat against the shore and go back and come again and go back...in the—endless dance of life.

I don't think any of what followed for the rest of all our lives could have been averted. It is spread over such a long time and time has snared so many people in its net that I don't know how anyone could have escaped the inexorable movement of the turning wheel.

What did happen was that Krishnan started coming first once, then twice, a week, then every day and many times my husband came in to find us together.

I wished he would stay away or go on tour so that I could have Krishnan all to myself. Sometimes we lay down together and he would do no more than kiss and at other times we would just lie there, in complete joy and his laughing voice would tell jokes and stories which just made me laugh. Sometimes he would talk of England and I would think, I must get there, somehow.

Who would have known, then, how I would get there!

He told me about the women who drank and smoked and he would light a cigarette himself. That my husband did not like. So it had to be done before he came. Many times I wanted to ask him about the landlady's daughter, but did not.

I was now in my seventh month of pregnancy. Father wrote and said I must come for delivery, Pati and my aunt would take care of me. The bangle ceremony and the seemantham, to mark the birth of the first child, had to be done. I packed my trunks and my husband took me to Delhi, where father lived.

I hadn't said goodbye to Krishnan. He hadn't come for over a week.

We reached and—can you believe it—I actually cried when my husband left. I would miss his help around the house. He had his uses.

Achyutan

Achyutan felt trapped. He had fallen in love with a girl who looked like a goddess but could not speak even one intelligent sentence.

Her smile was like a rainbow in a cloudy sky, her eyes were a beautiful smoky grey—where on earth had she got them from?—her figure made him pant.

And that is where it began—and ended. She had a repertoire of smiles, and each had its message—for him. Any attempt at conversation was met with monosyllables. She had no opinions, no thoughts, no arguments. It might make for a very peaceable life—or a deadly boring one. He must make up his mind.

The way the decision was made was a curiosity of Achyut's character. It summed him up. It was an impulse to beat all impulses, and it wasn't even about her.

It was a score he settled with Narayanan. It had to do with the journey to Melur, his banishment to his chitti's house, the part his father played in involving him with his mother's cremation, in some way Achyut had always felt that the cremation had resulted in the death of his mother.

They were on a trip to Madurai. Father and son made their way on the banks of the river of Madurai, Vaigai, and Achyut felt an old fear constricting him. Events that had happened many years ago, had not lost their intensity.

Here, he must break it here, he must tell him. No time to be lost, they had gone bride-viewing. Today he would decide whether a beauty without brains was better than the daughter of a distant cousin, a shy, dark girl who had never been farther than a day's journey from her home.

His old man—for he had always thought of him as such—walked in front, in a way that had become characteristic of him. Hands locked behind, a slow measured pace, hardly ever speaking. Following him, Achyut thought his father had become grayer since attaining grandfatherhood. Goutu had had a daughter and she had gone back to her home.

'What do you think about the girl' asked his father.

Now he must speak and he opened his mouth for the first words.

'Appa I have something to tell you…' he said.

Sometimes, inanities can presage profundities.

I can't imagine I actually married Savitri to spite Appa, but I think I did.

'I can't marry her,' I said. 'I can't marry anyone.'

'Why?' asked Narayanan. Was the boy going to become a monk?

'That is, except Savitri,' I said.

The old man stopped. So did I. 'Who is Savitri?' he asked.

Then the whole thing started. I can't remember the exact words now, but we got into a fight. Rather, I fought. The only thing he said was, 'She is very stupid. She may not even be able to cook.'

'Cooking doesn't need brains,' I yelled, 'anyway I am just informing you. I want to marry only Savitri.'

He muttered something about her stupidity. I must marry Savitri, this river is preventing rational thought. I haven't forgotten anything, you stupid old man. I haven't forgotten that I was cheated, lied to, that it was you and your decisions that changed the course of my life. Nothing is going to change it now. You make this marriage happen, go and grovel at Savitri's father's feet, the way I grovelled at my aunt's. It's your turn now!

Then we went back to Delhi and Father wrote some letter, I think, I've forgotten now, anyway Savitri and I were married. Goutu came back, baby in tow, she had to do the taali-*tying ceremony and her husband came with her. What did he say? Nothing, as far as I can remember, beyond a brief politeness.*

Then they all went back I can't remember where or how. All I know is I was making a grab for that beautiful body without a mind at every opportunity and pretty soon, the old man became a grandfather again. And again. And again. Many times over.

And in course of time, the old man moved to Madras. He said he couldn't stand the cold winters, but perhaps the frost in our home was colder than the winters of Delhi. It had something to do with his move.

I was left with the Beauty. The Beauty and the Beast. Yes, we made an odd couple.

Seshadri

'Goutu, Goutu.' Seshadri walked into the house and from the way he entered, the way he inflected her name she knew that there was News. She was not wrong.

'Goutami....'

'Coming!' she shouted from the kitchen. As she came out, he was pleased to note the way she looked but—wasn't it a trifle too flashy? Yes it was. The blouse was a little too low cut, the sari a little too clingy, her face a little too attractive. Her hair was black, but, and this made Seshadri frown mentally, it was due to a little lipsticky thing she used, only instead of being red, it was a greasy black.

She too was now the proud owner of a bureau which could be locked and Seshadri felt he did not know the contents of the bureau well enough. A man must know what was in his wife's bureau, it was like getting into the mind of his woman. It had been a gift from Narayanan on one of his visits to his daughter. She had been so pleased to get it that she couldn't stop laughing, and that evening they had has payasam as a celebration. Then the bureau had a pottu applied to it and camphor lights were waved so that the goddess Lakshmi, fickle as she was, would make it her abode. Seshadri had got a little angry with the enthusiastic reception the bureau had received.

Then and there the house had been rearranged. Things had been taken out of the two trunks and put inside the bureau. The bureau had two keys and this made its secrecy even more tantalizing. She would lock it with both keys and the ring would hang from her waist. That was another thing, everyone had to look at her waist, the keys gave her an air of importance which naturally drew glances from other men.

The bureau had marked a change in their relationship. He of the scientific temper could date the change from a slightly dependent Goutu to this self-assured creature who could lock things in her bureau and not speak about them, not leave them lying around in a trunk which anyone could open.

She need not explain the presence of things any more. She could keep them locked away inside her cupboard, inside her heart and mind. The thing that got him most alarmed was the possibility, no, the probability, of her having secrets inside the bureau. He looked away.

'I have got the promotion,' he said, but the pleasure he had felt as he had cycled along, faster than usual, had dimmed. 'We have to go to Delhi. That is where I am going to be.'

'What will you be?' asked Goutu. Her face was bright with excitement as she thought of her new status as the boss's wife. Seshadri had never failed her in his race to the top.

She hardly heard him. Her mind was full of the things she would tell her friends, the wives of the others who were here, on this far-flung outpost, manning the British government's excursions into power. The other wives better look out, she would be in charge. Her mind raced ahead, darting this way and that, from one thought to another, in the manner of a bird pecking at one fruit and then another. It was all exciting and pleasant.

Seshadri told her. They would leave in three weeks. The children were not in school. They would have to be put into schools in Delhi, they were old enough now. He had been teaching them himself, desultory lessons in English and arithmetic. In his considered opinion, they were not particularly intelligent and his seriousness grew when he thought of their schooling. He knew she was not thinking of this, she did not care about important, far-reaching things.

Seshadri stopped talking. He had meant to come in and make a dramatic announcement and all the way back he had imagined the little scene—Goutu and the girls arranged round him, a perfect portrait of family happiness, looking at him—and each other—with unalloyed joy, but the pure colours of the picture had faded, the light looked smudged, the dark a little more intense, as if a giant brush had been dipped in Indian ink and waved over the page. All his happiness had evaporated.

He took off his glasses and carefully cleaned them. The girls were standing at the entrance of the room, eyeing him guardedly. He had a sneaking suspicion that the girls were on their mother's side. His elder daughter was definitely on her mother's side, especially about the bureau. His face gained the expression, dark and brooding, of a storm. Goutu was very different from the girls of his village, she had a mind of her own but not a brain to match. So she was irrational and, to the logical Seshadri, irrationality fractured truth. It fragmented the action-reaction cycle and it mocked at the system which made for the process of thinking.

Busy in the kitchen, Goutu had gone several steps ahead, she had reached Delhi, the capital city of India, where they would now live. She saw herself, smartly dressed and confident, handing out tea and snacks to visitors, talking with them, impressing them with the depth and sweep of her knowledge. Then she would invite her cousins, ask them to bring the aunt in silks so that everyone would realize what they had missed. That would be the best revenge she could think of. It made her laugh out loud to think of it.

The only thought that came in to spoil this brilliant tapestry, like a black thread weaving a dragon in a scenery of fairies and goddesses, was that she would have to leave Krishnan. The connection was too strong, too near to her heart and life, it was the thread which bound her to that distant, tragic past where everyone important to her had gone away forever, not survived, left no trace of themselves behind for her to cherish.

Odd she did not think of Achyut, except fleetingly. Dharmakka came into her mind sometimes, but neither had been able to get her what she had wanted.

She had finished the cooking. Kitchen cleaned, she put the plates on the floor. Each had their own, Seshadri's was the biggest, a large silver plate with knobs on the underside so that it stayed off the floor and its impurities. The girls had their own plates.

When Goutu came in to tell Seshadri to come to have dinner, he was lying on the floor, in a posture which she hated, on his side, wearing only a veshti, bare-bodied, his poonool showing. He could not eat. He was moaning with pain. It showed in his eyes, which were flat and expressionless. After several attempts, she was able to make him rise, his slow walk and the way he sat on his palaha, putting one leg under the other in a deliberate movement, instead of just sitting, indicating how he felt. The atmospheric pressure in the kitchen rose. It was decidedly chilly and Goutu wondered what she had done.

She spoke very fast, as she always did, when his sudden darkening moods puzzled or frightened her, and the children became quieter.

So they all understood. Seshadri felt a glimmer of pleasure and satisfaction lighten his darkness. He started eating but would not speak, only make gestures to say he had enough.

'How is the rasam?' asked Goutu brightly.

No answer. He looked at her in the way he had, over the rim of his spectacles. He could see she was flustered and the children, scared.

Good. He had made his displeasure felt. No-one must take him anything but seriously. He was quite clear about that.

Goutu

When I look back at that time of my life, I feel as if I am slipping down a dark well, the dark well of time past, and in that dark, nothing is clearly visible. I have to hold up the dim light of a candle against the walls of the well, to see what I can snatch from its surface. That candle flickers and I go down, down, down, rushing through this spaceless, mindless dark, and sometimes, I see ghosts of people I think I knew—we were all girls and we are now old women, awaiting death, many have attained that state, only the other day I heard of Mangalam, and Sudha and Manorama.... The list is growing and I know that one day soon the name of Goutami is going to be added to it. Then the candle flickers—and dies....

What happened then was that I felt as if the heart had been cut out of my body, there it was, dripping blood and every drop had Krishnan's face on it. How dramatic and almost like a lie it sounds now!

But no dears it was not a lie then. It was the truth that I could not live without Krishnan, I who had to live with the death of so many members of my family, found it difficult to say goodbye to Krishnanand.

I think I made up my mind around that time that I would have to keep within myself some part of him that could not be taken away and would not ever leave me, a part that would remind both of us of the role each had played in the other's life.

For that was what it was. We were very important to each other. Valli and Narayani and the other cousins were all together, meeting, talking, laughing, having babies, fighting with their husbands, getting tortured by their mothers-in-law, but they shared a fate, a course. They heard the language of love from their mothers, Tamil, spoken with concern and care, even anger, giving advice, opinion, consultation.

Only the two of us were stuck in this northern climate, with its fearful, dusty summers, when the hot sandy winds from distant deserts blew fine grains into our eyes and mouths, making it impossible for us to speak, sometimes bringing a fiery darkness early in the noon, swirling patches of dust into our faces. And the winters, with the snow and ice and hail as big as potatoes falling with a thundering sound on our roofs, while I sat with the children in our small house, waiting for Seshadri's cycle bell to ring as he came down the lane.

Many times, he would be late, he had to take shelter in someone's verandah, and I, stiff with cold and fear, would imagine that Seshadri was lying dead, dead and frozen, down some ravine which he had not seen in the sleet and dark. The sound of the cycle bell would make me almost hysterical with joy and my elder daughter would go down and open the door for her father.

He would come up the stairs, tired and hungry and we would eat. He would mistake my joy at his presence for love and want to make love, or what he thought was love, and I would be furiously upset.

Are you asking how a girl, who had so little love in her life, knew so much of what she wanted?

I can tell you that now. I knew what love was even without being told or shown too much of it. It was a great pain and a total healing. All in one. And it was like another thing I had seen as a girl on the banks of Kolladam. Two little girls were crossing and suddenly the hot sands opened up and the girls were sucked into the water. None of us could do anything. They just went in. Yes, love is like that.

No, I could not be separated from Krishnan. He was the last connection I had with that distant childhood, unhappy as it had been, with no love, no care and no explanations, no teachings. He reminded me of the awful aunt, with her silks, the foxy Chitti who had reneged on my father, my mother and his mother and all the women who had died on their lying-in beds, leaving their children to the mercies of aunts who beat and stole and lied.

Funny that I did not think of my brother, Achyut who had given himself up to the beautiful Savitri's body as if it were a cause. Achyut had been the reason Krishnan and I had not married each other.

That was what I thought then. But now, as I sit back in my chair, my head resting on the wall, and try to hear the distant sounds of the past, I think I know why Krishnan and I did not marry. There were other scores life had to settle with the two of us, scores that gripped more innocent people than the two of us in its involved arms.

What accounts they were! To what distant places it took us! What is that sad face I see now in front of my eyes? My own? When I discovered what I had got into? Or Seshadri's, when he knew what I had got him into? Or the girls, scared and worried, wondering what was going to become of us all?

Or hers, who now sits before me, having given up every simple pleasure in life just to make sure I was not alone?

None of that old pleasure can I remember now. I am haunted by ghosts that rise and put out their tentacles to grab us all in their arms, pale and stiff. The passion is spent.

All that remains is the bitter taste of defeat. And I must wash it down before I die.

Seshadri

Seshadri started off to office at seven the next morning. His sorrow had not abated.

It had congealed into self-pity, hard and unyielding. His wife did not know how to serve him, her husband. She could not be contained, bound, by the rules of propriety. She laughed and talked and made friends very easily and she did not care who they were.

Seshadri had spent the whole of the night, body heaving with sighs, eyes filling with weak tears. He had gone to the bathroom many times, until Goutu was forced to wake up. She had just been lying there with her eyes closed, not sleeping, but she could not pretend any more. The bad 'mood', that was what she and her elder daughter called it, would last for a week until, tired and spent, she was ready to apologise any number of times, just to have him behaving normally.

When Seshadri was in one of his 'moods' the whole house would come to a standstill. He would, by some very clever verbal gymnastics, and she was no match for that, bring it round to her father and grandmother. His face would screw up into a frown and he would look out of the window as if drowned in sorrow and anger and Goutu would feel an old, familiar nausea rise in her, when the old silk hag shouted and she had nowhere to turn, nowhere to take refuge, except in lies.

That is how the brilliantly made-up lies had started.

If anyone had tried telling Seshadri that it was his inexorable devotion to truth that had made his wife a liar, he would have been shocked. Seshadri quite simply did not know how to lie. He considered anything other than truth, as he knew it, chaotic and therefore unscientific. It was not even a moral issue—it was purely a leading away, or being led away, from things as they were to what they might appear to be. He had never uttered a lie. He was not even conscious of this fact, it was to him like any other fact, merely a fact, something to be taken for granted, something to build upon, not to embroider. Beautifying things or rendering them more palatable did not even occur to him. Things could be made simpler, this meant more truth because truth was simple and the more profound and basic, the simpler.

No-one in his family lied. Not for them the shuttered veil of making things up to create an impression or escaping from trouble or not hurting feelings. They all spoke very little but when they did speak, it was to speak clearly and from the mind and the intellect. So when he met Goutu's natural ability of dissembling, first he was amused and then puzzled and, lately, angry.

It did not occur to him that, to Goutu, lying was as natural as telling the truth was to him. Her realities had to be spiced with the unreal, the grotesque, the surreal. It was not that she chose to lie over telling the truth. It was just that the first words she sometimes spoke were not factually correct. It was the same as the music she played, a song could be rendered in many ways without deviating from its basic structure, its raga.

On this morning, Seshadri turned over in his mind the alternatives he had. He could continue with the cold war or he could burst into flames and set the whole place on fire. The methods for both alternatives had been tested and found efficacious. If he went all cold, she would beg him to tell her what was bothering him and he would remain silent till she began to sob hysterically. He would speak in a cold voice, only in monosyllables until she, undone from the strain of it all, cried for hours. Satisfied with the effect, he would come back to normal the next day.

Then, the other way. He had shouted a few times, the girls would also get hysterical with weeping and all of them would be reduced to ashes by his rages, uncomprehending of what was happening to them. Then it would all die down, only to start over again a few weeks later. Both ways, he was very happy to see how pathetically grateful for the next few days they were to him for forgiving them

Yes, he had moods, and these rages he had were called—scenes.

I have a feeling she is cheating on me, thought Seshadri, with that cousin of hers. She thinks I don't know but I do. That is, I think I do. He is there too often and his wife has gone back to her father. I think they have been lying down together, though I don't know about sex. I have to find out, be sure before I confront her with proof.

That bureau has things in it that should be seen by everyone and I should have told her father to take it back.

Once we go to Delhi, I am going to tell her that the keys must remain hanging in the keyhole, anyone should be able to open it.

And in Delhi, people cannot visit the way they have done here. Maybe I will ask my mother to come and stay so that she can keep an eye on things. I must make sure that Krishnan does not come as often as he did here.

As he wheeled his cycle into his office, Seshadri felt better. He must now watch for results, the way he had watched over experiments as a student in the chemistry lab. Action would lead to reaction and time would tell. There could be no mistakes.

In the meantime, he would see his boss and start making his move to Delhi, the capital city, the centre of the rulers' power, where many, many cogs smoothly, or not smoothly, fitted into the larger wheels that made the government's machinery run without any major breakdowns. He was going there as one of the cogs, but with his application and his ability of getting to the heart of the matter, of splitting things up into their constituent parts and then putting them together again, much as a watchmaker makes watches, he knew he would become a wheel.

The boss, another Tamil-speaking bureaucrat like himself, looked at Seshadri. This man was going to make things happen, he thought, especially with a wife like Goutami. She was smart and had very few inhibitions. Quite attractive too. What was it he had heard about her and that Krishnanand? They were cousins, he had been informed. But what kind of cousins? But then he mustn't let these thoughts take over. 'You have two weeks' joining time, Sesh,' he said. 'You have to report on the 21st.'

'Yes, Sir,' Seshadri said. 'I'll be ready to leave.'

Then had come a discussion on what he must do there and Seshadri felt excited and happy. The unknown intellectual challenge always had the ability to do that. It was a pure cerebral rush that lit up his head and made his eyes, hidden behind those heavy, dark-rimmed glasses, shine.

'All right then,' said his boss. There had been a moment's hesitation. Should he, without informing his wife, invite Seshadri and his wife and the two daughters to lunch or dinner before they left? No, he dare not. His wife did not like Goutami, she was too friendly, had too much head-weight on account of her musical ability. Also, he thought of the cost of the dinner and decided against it.

'All right,' said Seshadri, a little self-consciously. Should he thank him? But for what? If he made too much of his part in the promotion, the boss might think he had done something special for him, Seshadri. That would be a grave mistake. Seshadri had got his promotion because of his hard work and diligence. No one had anything to do with it. He might think Seshadri was trying to flatter him and Seshadri didn't want that.

He made his way to the large room where he had sat for eight years and sat down. He was trying to collect himself. But before he could do anything with his racing mind, his colleagues had gathered round his table.

'Arre Sesh, tu to bada admi ban gaya,' said Shrivastav, his tea-drinking companion, in his usual loud, genial way. Mukherjee came and joined the group and looked forlorn.

'What about our table-tennis?' he asked. Seshadri and he played regularly. Seshadri did not reply.

He felt sad. He could not name this feeling. Companionable? He could not say. Feelings he had long learnt to ignore. They were not reliable indices of the mind. His mother, a woman of few words, had long ago taught her sons that. As a boy, he had been the most dutiful of her sons. He had divined her troubles but he thought they were her prarabdhams. Her good-looking husband, his father, was an adventurer. He loved travelling and on his return from his sojourns would very quickly impregnate his wife and his many brothers and sisters were the result of these couplings. It was left to him to take care of his mother when she reached the advanced stages of her many pregnancies and escort her to his grandfather's home in a nearby village. Then he would escort her back with the baby.

This routine had been disturbed when he had gone away to study. He had realized that unless he tore himself away from these beginnings, he would be doomed to stay in them forever. His beginnings were what was colourfully called humble, but he knew them to be poverty-stricken, deprived, difficult. Hunger had been a close companion, taunts and charity had provoked him to humiliated anger. He had resolved then to get away and the route must surely be through academic qualifications.

He had left that village home, with its soot-covered kitchen and dank walls and its only bed, far, far behind. There, too, he had left his feelings.

Shrivastav and Mukherjee were saying some more things to him when he looked up and saw, thankfully, his old classmates from college Padmanabhan and Sankaran approach. He jumped up with uncharacteristic enthusiasm.

'We came to congratulate you,' said Padmanabhan, in his deliberate, professorial way. 'Good work!'

Sankaran said nothing. He merely smiled. He thought of himself as an advaitin, and imagined that he viewed the pairs of opposites in the world with the same eye. His forehead was decorated with the sacred ash. Every morning he liked to remind himself that he too one day would be ash.

'So when are you leaving?' asked Padmanabhan.

'On the 21st,' said Seshadri.

'Not much time. How will you do the packing? Who will do it for you?' Padmanabhan rapidly fired these queries at Seshadri. He did not expect answers. Seshadri had learnt this the first week that they had been in college when he had asked him about his family and had not even waited for Seshadri's precise replies.

They all left. Seshadri looked at his watch. Six o'clock. He would go home. He had not thought about Goutu and the girls all day. All of it came flooding back but for some reason it had lost its pungency. He cycled home. Goutu was looking dull and sober, the girls were nowhere to be seen. He knew his elder daughter. She would have engineered this capitulation and told her mother how she must dress. All right, let them have it their way for now. He had a lot of other things on his mind, chiefly money. He must plan the move. All the rest could wait.

Goutu

You know, those days were very difficult. He was so suspicious and jealous. Now what is it I wanted to say? Let me think. Sometimes when I sit here and watch her difficult movements, her constant smile, her acceptance of her fate, I think, what might have happened if I, like her, had accepted my fate with better grace? Would she have been spared this birth? Would she have been spared all those years of dependence, of looking at others with a combination of pleading and innocence, trying to please, never disagreeing, because she knew how much she needed others?

I wish I had known this trick of acceptance. Because I did not accept my fate. I railed and broke free of all the rules that bound me to my special fate and wanted the life of another. I had made up my mind about what I was going to do. I was going to keep a part of Krishnanand for myself. I was not sure then how I was going to achieve this and the vague desire to remain with him had not yet become concrete.

Wait my dear. Don't think it was so easy. These dried up old breasts had plenty of desire in them, don't think they didn't. Sometimes now when I look at the TV, I think about how easy it is now to speak about all these feelings. But no-one gets it right. There is too much talk and too little feeling. Shall I try and tell you?

There is a feeling which is like the rise of a tide in the distant seas, which collects speed and more and more water as it moves. There is white foam and it rises higher and higher and comes into the shore and crashes. It hasn't lost its power, though. It goes flying back and while it goes back it meets with more foam and comes in, foaming and dangerous, with added strength and dashes on to the shore again, higher than ever. You could get carried away and you might return or you might not.

There is another feeling which is like the snows of these hills in which he and I and my husband lived, cold and distant, covering every bare branch with its weight, sometimes bending the branch so low that it breaks. There is no-one in sight, no-one who could take you back, were you lost, to the road. You might find it—or you might die.

Then, when I was a lost little thing, trying to survive with the aunt who would have me die, there was a river which was like a sea, so wide was it. Pilgrims came to its banks to visit, murmuring indistinctly, ashes and haldi and flowers, as if that had anything to do with faith-feeling, but the goddess in the temple, beautiful, dressed like a bride, resplendent with the praise and adoration of her devotees, would look on, impassive, unmoved. Dark it was in the inner room, suddenly that darkness would be lit up, momentarily, when camphor was waved on her face, up and down, her body for a second, then her feet and then the light would go out as suddenly as it had appeared and the priest would emerge from the dark into the light and we would all touch the light to our eyes and heads.

When the monsoon broke, with all its noise and light, the river would rise like a human being, it would have arms and legs like a rakshasi, so might Soorpanakha have approached the blue god, Rama, on his exile. She would swallow her daughter, the goddess in the temple, she would give birth to her again after the rains were over and she could reign on dry land again. I have watched it happen, you know, and thought then that this is how my mother was swallowed, but she did not come back. I have been swallowed too, and that is what I felt when I thought I would not see Krishnanand again.

So many times in my life, nearly over now, as I sit on this chair and wait for the minutes to tick away, and hear the clang of the bangle against the wheelchair's rim, I know that I was swallowed by feelings beyond myself.

No, no-one could have prevented the inexorable unfolding of events that happened, they were there like a series of events that happen every day, kalachakra, no-one can stop this wheel from turning and I don't believe that I could have stopped what happened any more than I could have stopped the sun from rising in the east every morning.

No, there was no stopping. There is no end, until death takes hold of us all.

She stands there, listening for the sounds of visitors, to relieve the burden of our lives together, lived over nearly half a century, across many continents. No-one, there is no-one there I shout, quietly she slinks away and stays in the shadows. That is what she was born to do, remain in the shadows for she was conceived in the shadows, the shadows of guilt and suspicion, of hasty and fearful and defiant lovemaking.

I look at her, so beautiful and true, tested by fire, coming through like a bright burnished golden Sita, who was found by the plough, daughter of the earth, suspected and deserted when her need was the greatest.

But my dear, at least in that I was better than the blue god Rama. I did not desert her.

Life in Delhi was tough. The summer heat was blistering and the winter cold freezing. By the time Seshadri moved into the quarters allotted to him he had worked himself up into a fine rage. The maddening expense of it all was poison. He could not think of anything else and it was only his work which kept him alive.

Goutu had no such misgivings. She swept, scrubbed, polished and washed. The floors shone like a mirror, reflecting all the small, simple things they had.

'We have too many things,' said Seshadri one day. 'Let us get rid of some of them.'

Goutu looked at him. They had been married for ten years and the strain of living with someone she only respected was beginning to show.

She now knew how other people lived. Sehsadri's position had brought them in contact with a class which put things and possessions first. She had swallowed her pride when some of her neighbours visited and she had to make them sit, South Indian style, on the floor on the pai. Her mind was filled with the thought of chairs and a sofa set. Beds too, and cots.

Too many things! They didn't have enough.

'I think we should have some chairs,' she boldly said. 'Maya knows a shop where she bought them really cheap….'

She stopped when she saw Seshadri's expression. Rage and disgust fought for place. They had two daughters. There were the school fees and the uniforms and all the other attached headaches. He also knew that she was getting some money from Narayanan. He thought she should give it to him, not keep it for her own vanities. The black lipsticky thing, which had now become a symbol of her desire to look young, came from that money as did the occasional choli. The cholis were stitched by a tailor who had a shop nearby and Maya had introduced her to him. Maya wore saris which he, Seshadri, disapproved of.

Also, Maya had a man visiting her when her husband was out. He had seen Goutu smirking with Maya at that man, who was supposed to be a famous writer. He was a Bengali and sang, and on one occasion, the violin had been brought out to accompany the harmonium which that madam played.

Prostitute! His mind had hissed. All laughing and talking!

And now she was going to change his home, his family values, his lifestyle!

'I will not have that woman in my house, do you hear me?' he shouted. 'She is a whore and she is making you one too!'

Goutu looked at him. In front of her eyes was not Seshadri but the bitch in silk, her diamond earrings shaking, sparkling in the sunlight, each shaft of light a sword, ready to strike, to kill. Her grandmother, still alive, was at this very minute being tortured by the bitch. Dharmakka had died on account of her.

Achyut had been sent away, she, Goutu, had no-one to call her own only because of that woman. The silk sari was shimmering, the diamonds, gleaming and mocking Goutu, daring her to take revenge. Well now she was going to take revenge. She was going to give it to her.

She stood in front of Seshadri. 'You call yourself a man?' she said. 'I think you are pitiful, trying to control me, when you can't control yourself at night, wanting sex all the time.'

Then it happened. He hit her and she lost balance. The gate opened and the girls came in, the elder one, laughing and talking, the younger one unsmiling and serious. They stopped when they saw her sobbing, holding her arm.

'Your mother,' Seshadri informed them in clear, ringing tones, 'is a a bad woman. From today she can't live in this house.'

The elder of his daughters was the first to reach her mother's side. 'Sit down,' she told her. She looked at him. The younger girl was instantly in tears, weeping silently, she couldn't move.

'Please say sorry ma,' the elder child begged.

Goutu was not sorry. The diamonds had stopped flashing and the silken back was retreating. Seshadri's face, contorted with anger, came into full view.Goutu was glad she had told her aunt off, it would make her think before she spoke. Seshadri or her aunt—it did not matter—she wouldn't be beaten.

Seshadri knew that the battle was out in the open.

Seshadri

Dear father-in-law, began Seshadri in his neat, beautifully-formed writing, Namaskarams.

I am writing this after much thought. Goutu has got out of control and is now treating me disrespectfully. She is talking about sex and other low things and is too friendly with a girl called Maya, who is our neighbour and who is teaching her bad things.

She is spending too much money and I feel you are to blame. You are sending her money secretly and instead of giving it to me for household expenses or saving it, as a good wife would, she is frittering it away on all kinds of things. I can't tell you what they are.

I strongly disapprove of your actions. I should have put my foot down when you gave her the bureau, that is when all this started. Now I feel you should send the money order to me, so that I can plan the expenses.

Expecting a favourable reply.

Respectfully,

S.K. Seshadri

He typed this out on his typewriter and he was careful enough to make a carbon copy to file away so that no one could accuse him of saying what he had not actually said. As he dug out a file to use, he found his hands trembling.

She had upset him. She had made him angry. He would not allow this to go on another minute. She must learn to obey and he would teach her.

What a fool I have been, thought Seshadri, not to have seen what would happen. Now I am sure she was having an affair with that cousin of hers and that is what is giving her the courage to speak to me like this. It was a good thing we got transferred to Delhi and they are not together. He is up there and we are here and it is not an easy journey. He will not take the trouble to come here.

He reached his office. The grand buildings, built by Lutyens, fringing the Viceroys' residence with their massive red and pink masonry had no effect on him. They shone in the winter sun and the tall Ashoka trees lining Kingsway, with India Gate at the end, the arches a perfect foil to the bleak winter landscape, left him unmoved. The trees shook their leaves, filigreeing in the winter sun. People were walking purposefully, wrapped in their winter clothes and he could get the enticing smells of food and tea from the stall near the *entrance to his office. There was his assistant, sipping tea from his saucer, smiling broadly; he didn't have a disobedient wife.*

Once inside, Seshadri almost forgot about his home. Only sometimes, he saw her flashing fire, standing up to him and he felt a sudden rage and depression. No Maya. No movies. He must stop taking her to their monthly treat, a movie and snacks at some hotel. The movies, with their songs and handsome men were beginning to give her ideas. As well as costing him money. Each movie meant about ten rupees expense. The elder girl was becoming too defiant, looking at him unblinkingly even when he shouted. Unafraid, she would give cool, logical explanations while the younger one looked scared and worried.

The whole thing would change. He dropped the letter into the post box and waited for it to fall with a satisfying thud as it joined the hundreds of letters fed into its belly. He could see his father-in-law, now completely gray, read this letter. He felt satisfied. He had done the right thing by telling her father. Letters were a good way to initiate action that was required, however painful the consequences. The demons of life were to be faced, the brutes, whatever turmoil they caused.

He thought of his own sister, in some deep dark village in the south and how he had had to rush to mediate with her husband and mother-in-law because she had not conceived even after two years of marriage. Her mother-in-law had accused her of not having the sex-organs of a woman, her son was pouring his seed into a nothingness. They had received just such a letter and he, a boy of twenty-one, still a student and home for the holidays, had had to go. His father was nowhere to be found.

Seshadri had been very stern on the occasion, 'You sleep with her,' he had said, 'don't you know whether she is a woman or not?' he had asked, sarcastically.

'Yes,' his innocent brother-in-law had answered 'but my mother says she is not.'

Seshadri had looked at his brother-in-law. The boy was a fool but he was a good boy.

'It is a son's duty to be kind to his parents and look after them,' he had finally said. 'But he has also got a duty towards his wife. It is yours to support your wife when people talk falsehood about her.'

His brother-in-law had looked away. His sister's mother-in-law had ranted and raved. His sister had locked herself in the lavatory and was threatening to commit suicide.

He had somehow managed to restore order and return to his own village. His mother, impassive and stoic as ever, was feeding the latest baby. She looked over Seshadri's head, saw that no-one was following him. So the affair had been settled.

'The food is in the kitchen,' was her only comment. The following year he had gone again to escort his sister home for her delivery.

The affair had indeed been settled.

Narayanan

Narayanan received the letter and noted its contents.

'Dear son-in-law,' he wrote. 'Well and wish the same with you. I read your letter. I am sorry Goutu is not showing you respect. I will write to her about the same. But I do not agree that the money I send her is for you. It is for her and the girls, if she wants to buy anything for them. I do not think you should want it. The bureau is for your clothes also. I will tell her to let you keep them in the bureau. If you want I will come to Delhi and tell her. If you let me know, I will book my tickets.

With regards,

K.N. Narayanan (father-in-law)'

Seshadri's face turned a dull red when he read this cheeky letter from Narayanan. 'Goutu!' he yelled.

The inner part of the house froze. She was playing her violin and as usual she had the two girls in attendance. Listening to the violin when the time would have been better spent doing some maths!

He heard the flurry of a violin case snapping shut and everyone scuttling.

'Here, read this.' He flung the inland letter in her direction. The moment was to return to her many times in life. Green, the colour of a leaf, the inland letter had been and, like a leaf, it fluttered towards her gently, zig zagging across the room. 'What does he think of himself?'

Goutu was puzzled. She lifted the letter and recognized her father's writing. Reading it she realized that her husband had written to her father. She looked at him.

'Yes, I wrote to your father.' Each word was clearly enunciated, the way Seshadri always spoke when enraged. 'I told him about your activities with men.'

There was silence. The walls of the house were readying themselves to absorb all that was now going to be said. Goutu braced herself, though the diamonds and the silk of her aunt's favourite sari were beginning to appear somewhere on the horizon. The intensity of the silence was stretching her nerves taut, and twisting them this way and that, in quite the same way as she twisted the clothes when she wanted the last drop of water wrung dry. Outside somewhere she could hear a bird calling and children's voices, clear and high and shrill, over the silence.

Still silence. So he was not going to tell her what activities with men he was talking about. Then what was it she heard, some droning in the background, some words spoken in a language she did not know, who was speaking and what were they saying?

Something about her being thayilla, motherless. And she was kicking and screaming and her cousins were laughing and looking excited and happy, Dharmakka looking serious.

She forced herself to listen to what the clear enunciation conveyed.

'He can't come here again,' it was saying. 'I will not speak to your father ever again. He has insulted me and he thinks I am after some pittance he sends you. My principles forbid me to allow him here or to speak to him or have you and my daughters having anything to with him. Do you understand?'

She stood there, stock-still. The verbal bullets had stopped firing. It had turned its back and was walking purposefully away.

So that was to be the end of her father's visits. He must not come here again. She turned and went back to the inner room, where the girls were cowering. Her elder daughter understood, teeth clenched, the younger one stood petrified.

Her last connection with her home was being severed. She corrected herself. There was still one more connection. Her mind was now resolute. That was not going to be broken whatever anyone did. She would make sure of that.

Goutu

Well, what would you do? I am putting this question to my granddaughters, yes I have two, beautiful girls they are too.

Oh ammamma, we would kill our husband, says one.

I will shoot him says the other.

I will throttle him says the first one.

Now it has become an argument about how they would put an end to their husbands if either dared say a thing like this about their fathers.

Lovely, girls! I say. Let us practise. We all laugh.

That is what time does, the kalachakra which spins without anyone having to turn it.

At the time I did not laugh. But, strangely enough, neither did I weep. Something was happening inside of me. Can I tell you what it was? Will you listen to me?

There are lots of ways I could describe this to you. Have you ever seen the way rice and dal get ground for dosa? Gada gada goes the fat stone against the grinding stone. And after about an hour's hard work, the paste is ready. Then comes the part of making the dosas, sizzle, sizzle the oil around the batter on the frying pan. I was sizzling and no-one knew.

Then have you seen anyone laying roads in the sun? Do you know how hot tar is poured on the road and it hardens and in a few days even a bus can go over it, it is so hard. I was that hot tar hardening.

Things were shifting inside me, like you shake a bottle so that more can fit into it. I was going to fit in more things into my life and no-one was going to stop me. Not my father and certainly not the father of my children.

My life was going to take another course. Up in the Himalayan ranges, I had seen many small streams, winding down after the snows had melted, going down, sparkling in the sunlight, sometimes reflecting the dull gold of the moon as we had gone back walking. Clear waters they were, glacier-cold from the places where they had taken birth and then, they would join the mighty Ganga, the mother of Bhishma. Lovely names those streams had, the Alaknanda, the Kalindi. And later, as life took us from one part to another, I saw that when a river takes its own course, it becomes very fertile, a life-giver.

I was going to become one of those streams. My life was going to take another turn. Ah me, if I had only known what a turn it was going to take!

No, even then I would have done exactly what I did, there was no going back after this.

I was sizzling and I had hardened. Now I would have to act. Krishnan would not be banished from my life.

Seshadri

The girls were in school and doing reasonably well. But according to Seshadri, neither had the scientific temper required for intellectual competence. The elder of his daughters had a lot of courage, he had to grant her that, but not detachment. They were all too attached to the consequences of their actions, and since by his fortieth year, Seshadri had begun to fancy himself an ascetic, he felt a thrill of pride in his own superior spirituality.

His wife, on the other hand, was full of little religious rituals, the lamp had to shine like burnished gold, the wicks had to be hand-rolled, the girls and she spent a full hour on Sunday mornings, precious study time, rolling out wicks from his old veshtis, it used to drive him silently mad as he watched. First, one of them would tear a piece off and then it would be made into thin strips, each one rolled carefully and placed into a sweet box with the word Cadburys written on it. He had bought a box of chocolates when he had made one of his trips to Calcutta, his work was taking him places and he quite enjoyed all the attention he was getting. He remembered the excitement surrounding the box when he returned.

'Oh Appa,' said the younger of his two daughters, 'what a lovely box!'

Such was her innocence that she did not think it contained anything.

'Open it,' ordered her elder sister, and made a grab for the box. Goutami came out, her head tied in a towel.

'Give it here,' she said, in a high strident tone. Seshadri was surprised. Her voice was becoming unwomanly, it had lost its grace, there was no quietude in her voice or face. It was looking for something.

The girls had obeyed instantly, that was one thing he liked in her, she managed to control them with a look, a whispered imprecation, a quick but hard pinch on their arm or thigh. They were not allowed to scream, they were instantly silenced.

The chocolates had been rationed and had lasted about two months. Then the box had been cleaned and used as a wick box.

Seshadri refused even one chocolate, they were an indulgence which he considered loose. He was an ascetic, in mufti.

Two years had passed and Goutami and he had settled into a state of uneasy truce, he, suspecting her fidelity and she, hating his money-grubbing. She had a large group of friends and had learnt to speak Hindi with the ease of a native. She would go out with them and on certain evenings, upon returning home, Seshadri would find some new addition in the house, a cushion cover, a bed sheet or a new utensil. So Narayanan was still sending her an allowance.

He sometimes regretted, for he was a just man, his pronouncement about her father. He had acted too quickly. There was a Tamil saying that an angry man loses control over his buddhi, his discrimination. Yes, that is what had happened. It was too late now. It was not proper to concede to one's wife that one had got carried away. To say sorry was out of the question.

Perhaps at some time in the next few months, he could casually say, 'Why don't you invite your father for the child's birthday?' Or Diwali or vishu. How grateful she would be! A grateful Goutu would be delectable! Seshadri grew sentimental at the thought. Yes, he would do that.

Folding his paper, he got up. The wick-making ceremony—for that is what it was—was also over. He took off his spectacles and rubbed oil on his glistening black, thick hair. Goutu had often told him that it was she, not he, who should have such a head of hair.

He smiled at the girls. 'Let us go for a walk to India Gate,' he suggested.

'Oh Appa, we have homework,' they cried. 'Let us go in the evening'.

'All right,' he answered. He looked at his second daughter, sweet child, he thought. So quiet, like himself. If only she didn't break into sobs so quickly. There was something nerve-wracking about the way she wept.

That evening they went to India Gate. They walked up and down and then Seshadri broke his rule and unbent sufficiently to buy them all some snacks at the chanawala's. They sat there, munching, the girls playing some imaginary game, Goutu and he looking for all the world like an ordinary husband and wife.

He watched her popping the chanas one by one into her mouth, quite sweet she looked and he looked at the girls. He felt content. All that was required was the opportune moment when he could reinstate his father-in-law into his wife's life. He had been precipitate there, there was no getting away from that and she had not asked even once whether her father could come. He knew there were letters and—irritating thought—some money.

Suddenly, there was a flurry of activity. It was Kamala, a distant neighbour and her large brood. They were all making a beeline for them. Sehsadri got up. He didn't quite like the way she carried herself, she was loud and talkative and had too much to say about her father's house in Madras. He had heard it all. It was an old house in a bylane in Mylapore, within harking distance of Kapaleishwarar temple, they could see the gopuram in all weathers. Gopura-darshanam it was called and it was almost as good as going to view the lord everyday. She had done the matric examination—Madras matric, not Andhra matric—when the proposal had come from her husband's family. Her grandfather had said she could not study any more, it was a waste for one destined to spend a lifetime in the kitchen. So she, like many others had come to Delhi, leaving behind gentle Madras, with its fragrances and sweetnesses, its hot summers, followed by evening rain, a gentle drizzle which sensuously assailed the nostrils with the smell of wet earth. And its beach, with the sea beating on the shore, a free outing for all Madras dwellers. There you could buy for a pice a small paper cornet full of a delicacy called shundal, bits of mango it had, interspersed with small pieces of coconut. You could play and sit and talk, and the little girls, some of the bigger ones too, wearing their gaily coloured pavadais, would hold hands across and turn round and round until their skirts were a mad whirl of colour. Flushed and laughing, covered with sweat, they would fall on the sand, in ecstatic exhaustion, only to rise a moment later and begin all over again. They would walk back home and have their sand-covered hair combed out before going to sleep on their mattress-rolls spread on the floor. You didn't need the kind of beds a north Indian winter dictated, there was something almost pure in those rolls, she said, she would just get up and be awake.

All that Kamala had left behind to come to Delhi, and like Seshadri, her husband, Natarajan, had left his village home many, many years ago and in his home there were, as in Seshadri's, many little parcels of memory, little parcels, tied up carefully with string and put away somewhere deep, deep down. These were not wilfully ever brought out, but sometimes they had an inconvenient way of popping open and had to be tied up again. A man given to few words, already balding, though only his, Seshadri's, age.

His greeting was a Tamil noise, made from the nose. 'Uhn, uhn,' he said and smiled.

All the five children were there, dressed in the same way, the two boys wearing shirts made of the same material exactly as the girls' dresses.

'Meet Kamala's brother,' said Natarajan. 'He is staying with us for a few days till he finds a job. Subra, this is Seshadri and his family. They are our friends.'

The man called Subra held out his hand. 'Subramaniam,' he said in a deep voice. 'Pleased to meet you.'

Seshadri was surprised out of making a namaskaram. He dropped his hands mid-air and took the proffered hand and smiled.

Goutu and the girls watched, fascinated. The girls edged closer, they had never seen a handshake in action, only in the movies, and they were thrilled with his voice, his English accent.

Kamala looked on, proud of the stir her brother had created. 'He has just returned from Germany,' she said. 'He was in the Army.'

'What do you do now, Mr Subramaniam?' enquired Seshadri.

'Oh call me Subra,' said Subra lightly. 'I joined the army at the beginning of the War and now that peace has been declared, I have been demobbed. Out of work!' He laughed.

Seshadri's daughters were round-eyed. Goutu got up. This man was worth looking at. She liked the way he spoke and she liked his laugh. There was very little laughter in her life. He was tall and well-built and he moved with what she felt was the grace of a soldier, used to the hard life. No-one knew that he had been dishonourably discharged.

'My wife Goutami,' briefly said Seshadri. He wished with irritation that she hadn't risen from the lawn, they would have gone away taking this man with them.

He hoped Subra wouldn't put out his hand to Goutu. He didn't. But what he did do was even better. He looked at her directly and said 'Namaskaram,' and smiled. Goutu was transfixed, she said nothing. She was watching his teeth, even and white and thinking that he was the second most handsome man she had ever seen.

Then there were some more pleasant exchanges and Kamala moved on. The moment had passed, or so it seemed. Seshadri and Goutu walked home with the two girls. Goutu went into the kitchen and started heating the food

They had dinner and as the fitting end to a perfect day, Seshadri reached over for his wife when he thought the children had gone to sleep and they had sex, Seshadri's body with Subra's face.

Or was it Subra's body with Seshadri's face? Goutu couldn't tell.

Goutu

No I couldn't tell my dears. When did this devil enter my mind and heart? The devil which whispered all sorts of things to me, things that I feel ashamed to think of now, after over fifty years! Yes, fifty years it is since I met Subra and that long hot summer when I was cheating on my husband every opportunity I got. It didn't make me happy you know, it made me even sadder with my life and all the things I had missed.

Anyhow, what happened was that one day as I was taking the girls to school, I heard someone say hello to me at the bus stop. I stopped dead. I had heard the Voice only once but it had got stuck in my mind. I turned around, pretending to be surprised. I wasn't really. I knew who it was. It was Subra.

'Do you drop them everyday?' he asked.

'Not everyday,' I replied. 'Sometimes when I go to the market.'

'Oh,' he said. That was all.

But he was there again and again. And again.

I would be carrying a heavy bag of vegetables and he would offer to carry it for me. 'This is not ladies' work,' he said. I didn't understand. Then whose work was it?

'Men's', he said. 'Women are to be taken care of, like flowers.'

Then on the fifth or sixth accidental meeting, he suggested that we have a cup of tea at the shop near the vegetable shop. Lots of people were standing there drinking tea from their saucers. I thought it was safe and even if anyone saw me, I could pretend to be alone. He paid for both of us.

We had the tea and he walked right up to the square outside our house with the bag. I was scared out of my mind. My neighbours would snigger.

In course of time, I had to tell Maya. 'At last,' she said. 'Your husband is a funny man.'

I stopped going for a few days. I was too afraid. But one morning he came right up to the house. The doors had iron bars and you could easily see who was standing outside.

I rushed to open the door. Part of me was thrilled and the other part afraid.

'Shall I come in ?' asked the Voice.

I said nothing. He came in through the open door and I standing there like one made of stone.

Then the thing started. Lies and deceit and more lies and more deceit. Then taking money from me because 'my pension is slightly delayed, I get paid from England, you know,' or 'Kamala wanted some money so I had to give it to her.'

'This is not wrong. We love each other and love is not wrong,' was his constant answer to any guilt I felt.

When the children came in I would hug them to me, they were the only real thing in all this madness, this unreality, this make-believe. They were quite surprised, I think, at this show of affection. They were only used to slaps and pinches and shouts. For the bitch in silk had infected me enough. All I had got from her were slaps and beatings. So I was passing them on.

I didn't know all this then, dears, or perhaps I wouldn't have done it. Now as I sit here though I know that the real thing is all illusory. I acted that way because there were other fates playing with mine. All those fates had to be played out too, other lives had unfinished business which my actions had to finish for them.

Or how would you account for the things that happened then? I even gave away one of my necklaces because his money had not arrived on time from England. Then those lies about the necklace. I lied so much that on some days I think I told no truths.

When my husband came in every night, I would go out of my way to be cheerful and even I knew how I was behaving. He would look at me carefully, my heart would go dung, dung in my breast. Could he read my mind?

The truth came out in a way I least expected. Though I should have known with my husband's fondness for letters that it would come this way.

One morning, Subra was sitting in our inner room as he did and I was making some coffee, when there was a knock. I went to open the door.

No, this could not be true

It was my husband.

'Do we have a visitor?' he asked laughing unpleasantly.

Subra came out.

'I was passing this way,' he said. 'I thought I would say hello to your family.'

'More than just hello,' said Seshadri, his voice rising. 'You have been a visitor here for over two months.'

'I think there's been a mistake,' said Subra in his smooth way. 'I haven't been here for about a month now.'

Then Seshadri took out a bunch of letters.

'Dear Mr S,' they said, 'do you know what your wife does when you are at work? Don't you want to?'

Each of those letters was dated and the details were graphic. Only they were unsigned.

'Anonymous?' said Subra loftily, trying to bluff his way out of it. 'I don't think it would hold much water in a court of law.'

'Get out of my house,' said Seshadri, icy with anger, his voice a mere whisper. 'But before you go, return my wife's necklace.'

So he knew about that too! Goutu was breathless with fear and pain.

'I've sold it,' said Subra. 'A man's got to live, hasn't he?'

Goutu looked at him, breast heaving. So he had cheated her. There had been no pension, no loans to Kamala. He was a liar. That was a necklace belonging to her mother, one of the few that had been salvaged from the ruin of the chitti's house. It was gone and this man had done it.

She broke into loud wails then, the sobs racked her body as if it was her mother, and not just her necklace, she was mourning, the grief came over her in waves and all the many things that she had loved and lost came to her in waves which sucked her under, stifling her life breath, threatening to kill her, spraying her nose and eyes and throat with the salt of the sea of grief—tears in which she was drowning. She heard herself then, her voice a shrill uprising of dukham and suddenly she was being rained with blows and Seshadri's voice over hers, unrecognizable with anger and impotent rage and misery, coming in short spurts, dying out and picking up again till she thought she must surely die.

Later in the evening, grief spent, she sat in a corner. The children had come in from school, Seshadri lying in bed and the girls too afraid even to speak. The elder girl watched for a while and then she walked up to her father.

'What has happened, Appa?' she asked.

Seshadri turned, his eyes filled with tears.

'Your mother has ruined all of us,' he said. 'We can't live here anymore. We have become the joke of the neighbourhood.'

The girl turned to her mother.

'You are supposed to be doing something good for us,' she said, 'but all you do is fight and make things difficult. Can't you behave yourself?'

Goutu reached out and gave her a slap.

'Yes hit me,' said the girl. 'That's all you can do. Hit and slap and pinch.'

Was she talking to her or was she, Goutu, saying it to her silk and diamond aunt?

Seshadri got up from his bed. 'From today don't touch my children,' he said. 'You have lost the right to touch them. I don't want them becoming like you. I will write to your father and ask him to take you away. I will look after the children with my mother's help.'

So again it was to be a letter that changed the course of her life. Goutu said nothing.

He turned and went into the kitchen. The three of them sat around the plates, her second daughter a picture of misery.

She sat in her corner all night. The morning found her lying there, curled into a ball. The children had gone to school and Seshadri was nowhere to be seen. Had they eaten anything? She picked herself up, every bone and sinew and heartstring in acute pain.

The letter. That would take her away from the children and everything she called her home.

Goutu

I told you it was the red sari, made of georgette that had done all this. No one knew that I had bought it on my outing with Maya. It was a shop in Connaught Place and she wanted to go to buy some lace for her petticoats. Maya did all sorts of things like that, things which would make me excited and afraid at the same time. Under her blouse, she wore—a bra she called it. It made me shy just to look at it. Those thin straps holding up two breast shaped cups! I was so nervous when she wore it in front of me, I said, 'Stop, stop,' though I couldn't help but admire it.

'Why don't you buy one?' she asked, giggling. She knew what would happen if I bought one of those.

'Your husband may get ideas,' she remarked, giggling some more.

I got up. I mustn't stay here and listen to any more of it, I thought. Just then the doorbell rang and, still clad in her bra and petticoat, she flung a duppatta over her breasts and went off to open the door. It was the Bengali boyfriend.

'Arre Maya, kotho shundor, ahaa,' and the rest was lost in giggles.

I felt I had heard enough. I admired Maya but even I felt the gulf between us.

But when next time, she passed my house she asked if I would come to a shop to buy lace, I thought it was all right. So off we went.

The georgettes were hung in front of the shop and swirling colour in the wind like that, they were beautiful. There were pinks, which looked wonderful when North Indian girls wore them with their fair skins, and greens, shining like pachai-kallu.

But it was the kempu colour that caught my eye. Deep, deep red, arrakku was my favourite colour in saris. I had many of that colour, even now I do, I know how well it suits me.

I looked up at the hanging sari, going round and round in the wind, a maroon balloon, beckoning me.

Maya watched me. 'Buy it,' she said. It is only fifteen rupees.'

Fifteen rupees! I laugh when I think of it now. It was what I spent on the house for the whole month. No, I could not. There would be too many questions.

'I'll lend you the money,' said Maya. 'You can pay me later.'

So the sari was bought, my heart beating with fear and guilt, and hidden under the bottom shelf paper of my bureau.

It was many months before I wore it. The first time was when I went to pick up the children from school. I felt like a thief, but an excited thief.

I paid Maya three rupees a month for five months. The Bengali boyfriend knew and he laughed. 'Becoming a dushtu, ha ha,' he said. 'We are converting you!'

When I arrived in school, my daughters rushed passed me, they didn't know me in that sari. 'Amma, what is this?' asked the younger one.

The older one was more brief and to the point. 'Does Appa know?' she asked.

I glared at her and she was silenced. The next day, she was hanging around me before she left for school.

'Amma, that sari,' she began.

I turned on her. 'If you mention that sari in front of your father,' I said in my most frightening whisper, 'I'll slap you. Do you hear me?'

'Please don't wear that to school, Amma, please, please,' her voice trailed off. Even she had tears in her eyes.

I just shot out my arm and gave her a slap.

She left without a word, shoulders heaving.

Well my dear, that's the way it was. I wonder where it went, that mischief-making sari, I can't even remember. Must have been given to the vessel seller in exchange for a kinnam or karandi. Or maybe when we finally moved, I gave it to the maid.

Because we did go from there. I had disgraced all of them. I had been caught with a man inside my house when my husband was away. My husband wouldn't even go for his walks. He stayed inside after coming from office and there were fights and fights and tears and accusations. One day the doorbell rang and my father entered. He stood at the door and struck his head with his hand.

'You have made me ashamed,' he said. His suitcase was on the doorstep. Someone brought it in. My legs were not holding me up, I was having a stomach pain. My husband had tears in his eyes and the girls were sobbing.

'Son-in-law, if you think I should take her back with me, please say so.'

My husband said nothing.

Wild hope entered my heart. Was I to be forgiven then? Could I stay with the children?

'She has disgraced me and your family,' said my father. His hands were folded, like a namskaram. 'As you are such a great man, please forgive her,' he said.

Now it has all become a blur, so how do I remember all this? My dear, I remember all this and more. I even remember how many different things I felt, standing there in that little room, doors tightly locked, so that the neighbours could not look in.

Let me tell you. I felt empty, something like the feelings when Krishnan had been sent down the stairs by Achyut just before my wedding. As if my life had come to an end. Then I felt deep sadness that I had done this to my children and, yes, to my husband. I felt hatred for Subra who was nothing but a liar and cheat. But then so was I. So did everyone hate me in the same way?

And then I felt something for my father and his namaskaram which I don't know to describe even now.

He stood there with his hands folded for about five minutes. My husband still did not speak.

Seshadri

Even years later, Seshadri did not quite know why he had acted the way he did. Was he such a weakling? Was he not a man? Then why did he let her stay?

The fact was, he told himself, he was a noble man. It was noble of him to let her stay, let her cook for him, clean after him, wash his clothes, look after his children, in later years, ride with him in a car, go out with him to all those functions and parties, let her keep a beautiful house. Yes: he was a punyamanithan.

His father-in-law had stood there, broken and defeated, talking about her being thayilla, motherless. He had wept and sobbed and Goutu had stood there like one made of stone, watching her father. The next day he had left, before leaving, he had held both Seshadri's hands in two of his and taken them up to his forehead, in a gesture of the most abject worship. So might a mere mortal supplicate Mahavishnu, if He, the indweller of all, deigned to show him a vision as a boon for many years of tapas. Then he had left, a bent old man, carrying a trunk. Goutu had held her sari end to her mouth, to prevent herself from crying out loud.

Then he had asked for a transfer, it was suicidal, he was being groomed for higher things. Independence had just been granted, the horrors of Partition were behind them and he was in the new capital, under everyone's eyes. And he, asking for a transfer! Delhi, heaved and shaken under the earthquake of violence and mindless killing, refugees and immense heartache and sorrow, was slowly getting another hue, one brightened by the optimism of the new citizens.

All the time when her own life was turning upside down, Goutu had been almost oblivious to the changes that had been happening around her. There was talk of Gandhiji and Jinnah falling out and everyone said that India would be split into two. Goutu didn't believe them. She knew, as everybody else did, that Gandhji would never allow such a thing to happen.

Long, long ago, Gandhiji had come to Rajahmundry, where her uncle had been an engineer and all of them had gone to catch a glimpse of him. He had a high-pitched voice and they'd watched him, round-eyed and breathless. He said he needed women to help them in the struggle. One of the men in her family—a distant cousin who, it was said, had been in love with Narayani but feared her uncle who would have shot him first and asked questions later—had joined the struggler and spun the charkha everyday. It was rumoured that Gandhiji did not approve of men and women sleeping together even if they were married. Someone started a collection and when the plate had come around and people were putting money into it, Goutu had slipped off one of her bangles and watched it clang into the plate. It was her bit for the country.

Now this talk of Muslims leaving and going to a new country and the Hindus from there coming into India—but what was the new country? It was all one country. She had friends, her neighbours, who said their parents were in Lahore, in Karachi, in Hyderabad. She even knew people from Madras who lived there. It was impossible to comprehend what was going on,

One day it was brought home to her quite powerfully. Down the road from her, in a quadrangle exactly the same as hers lived a Muslim family. The daughter-in-law, Halima, was a wonderful knitter and many times Goutu had gone to have a pattern explained. Soon after the rumours of Partition gained ground, Goutu went to Halima expecting the same warm welcome she had always got.

She was turned away at the door—she could see Halima at the rear of the house, but her father-in-law told her that she was not there. He looked very angry, and Goutu turned away, not understanding. A few days later, she was buying milk and she saw the whole family leave.

They had gone to Pakistan.

All the time, when her life was undergoing such changes, when she was discovering whether anyone approved or not, while she was realizing that she was a beautiful accomplished woman, the world around her had been changing.

Seshadri did not think that the changes imminent in the world outside should mean a reassessment. He would remain himself—honest, integral, unified. He knew that that there were going to be cataclysmic changes in the fabric of society as they had understood it. He saw, that for all that the British had appeared to respect Gandhiji and even held him in awe, they were not going to leave without the overt stamp of their governance, which was to divide and rule. He had absolutely no illusions about the whites. He did not think, as did a lot of his anglicised colleagues, that they belonged to a superior culture but he admitted that they had the one thing he valued the most—the scientific temper.

Delhi had become a hotbed of rumour and so he often thought of sending Goutu and the children to Madras where they would be safe while he continued in Delhi till the storm had passed, leaving god only knew what debris. For debris there was going to be, that was clear with each passing day. Already, he was hearing of arrivals of trainloads of people who were coming away before the final blow fell, though no one quite knew when that would be. Goutu had had conversations with many, of course, before the Bengali boyfriend arrived to claim her, laughing as he always did at the puritanical Tamil girl sitting with his lush Maya. Then Maya would go inside the bedroom with him and Goutu would leave: they were so open about their affair of the body and Maya told her this.

'Sex is wonderful,' Maya had said, 'I don't think you know what you are missing.'

Goutu had stared at her.

So the conversations of what might happen if India was divided—no one heard of the word Partition since it hadn't been coined—were brief. But Khudiram—for that was the boyfriend's name—spoke about it once, and once only.

His family were in Chittagong. He and Maya had just finished their riotous bedroom act and Maya was still in her blouse and petticoat when Goutu knocked at the door.

'Everyone is saying that India is going to be divided', she said. 'What will happen, Khudida?'

Maya was looking for something in a box, her back turned, her hair partially covering her face. Her voice was muffled.

'Arre, nothing will happen,' she said, 'the rents will go up. There will be crowds of people everywhere.'

Khudiram looked down at his hands, not speaking for a few minutes. He didn't look at either of them, but Goutu got a glimpse of his face. She saw the expression: bitter, tired, taut, drawn, full of an unspoken anger.

When finally he spoke, his voice was different, full of impotent rage.

'There will be bloodshed like we haven't seen before,' he said, 'women will be raped, men will be killed, children will be orphaned. There won't be homes, people will have to do things they don't even know about, dying of hunger.' His voice trailed away. 'My parents are in Benaras now,' he said. 'My mother is doing stitching, my father has lost our house and all his land. They are all in one room, with my brothers and their wives. My sisters are with my aunt in Calcutta. I try to send as much money as I can from my writing, my tuition and music classes.'

Maya had stopped her search She had turned round and was looking at him, her eyes wide, a predator's expression on her face.

'You said you were the son of a rich man who owned land in Chittagong,' she said. 'You cheated me!'

Goutu, too, stared at him, but for another reason. She had not seen this side of Khudiram. Maya went and sat down in a chair, the very same one that Goutu had admired and desired.

'Arre, ki holo, esho, esho.' Khudiram said, trying to bring it round to their usual sexual banter. But Maya would not be comforted. Khudiram got up from the couch, a lit cigarette in his hand. He looked down at her for a few moments, and put his hand on Maya's hair. She slapped it off. He took away his hand and went down the corridor to the front door. They could hear his chappals flapping against the floor. Maya was sobbing openly now. Goutu couldn't bear to look at the sight.

'Maya,' she began. Maya did not answer.

Goutu left.

What can I say of what happened next? There are no words to describe what we went through. As I sit here, so many years after Partition, as we all came to call it, the images are still fresh in my mind. It was exactly as Khudida had predicted, only a hundred, no, a thousand, times worse. There was killing and there were rivers of blood. As we lay in bed at night, in our houses, no one knew what might happen. All the menfolk, including my husband, had to take turns in guarding our homes. We would hear their sticks beating the ground and more chilling than anything else were the cries that resounded in the night—'Allahu Akbar' with a return cry of 'Har Har Mahadev'.

I did not sleep for months. I did not sleep for nights. Calcutta was crushed with people, people and more people. There were families arriving every hour and there were days when we could not go even to the shops. The girls had stopped going to their new school after an incident when the younger one darted out of the house and the elder one went running after her.... I ran after them like one crazed. Only yesterday there had been news of children being put into drums of hot oil, dying a slow and painful death. And my daughters—someone would spoil them. We didn't use the word rape, it was too non-committal. They would be spoiled, spoiled for their husbands. As I stood there, tears streaking down, someone brought them back.

I slapped both of them as we ran back indoors.

'I wanted to see Appa,' the younger one said, 'and she said all right, go'.

''That was because you were boring me the whole afternoon about Appa!' the elder one shrieked.

Their father had started growing a beard and stayed in a friend's house near the office. I didn't know for days at a time whether he was alive or dead.

Phones? No, my dear, there were no phones, not in out house anyway. But I had seen them, you know, you picked up the top part and told someone the number you wanted and after some time, you might hear the voice you wanted to hear.

So we knew what was in store for us. I might have become a widow for all I knew. I would crush this thought as soon as it came to my mind. No, I did not love him, but the thought of going back to my father's miserable house, where he lived broken-down and defeated,was ubearable. My brother Achyut had left his wife, rather she had left him with her many children. My father had stopped speaking about anything. He would nod and smile, but the sadness stayed. The house, with its cramped windowless rooms, its womanless sorrowful air, would kill me.

Sometimes, the old times came back to my mind, when as a newly married girl I had lain awake at night, after my husband had claimed my body in a brief ritual of copulation, when I had missed my father painfully and sharply. I remembered the first time I had wanted him to visit. My husband was reading the papers, I cleared my throat, it was the signal that I wanted to say something. No, I could not call him by his name.

'Hun,' he said absently.

'This is such a beautiful place,' I started.

'What do you want?' he asked, putting down his paper.

'Shall I write to my father and ask him to come here?'

'My mother must come first,' he said. 'I am planning to go and bring her. There is a right way to do things. Naturally my mother must be the first visitor.'

I turned away. My father could not come. He must not be the first visitor.

'My father is going away to find a new job,' he said, 'She cannot be alone in the village. So she will be with us for a few months.'

And later, I had had to ask him for a postcard to write to my father. I had to show my letters to him and he would correct the spelling. He would also change what I had written. It was part of doing the right thing.

But now I did not want to go back. I had left it all behind. Subra had shown me that I had powerful emotions and Maya had changed my ideas of right and wrong. I had become hard, yes dears hard

There was one part alone that I sometimes brought out, just as a miser may examine his small hoard of gold. That was when I thought about Krishnanand. It was he who had the power still of taking me back to that old Goutu who kicked and shouted and fought, who had feelings about others.

Krishna and Sridevi had also gone their respective ways, she back to Madras and the grand old house and he? I didn't know. I had all the gossip that came out of their comings and goings. She had come for a holiday and never gone back.

He had never gone asking for her.

He had stayed on in that distant mountain fastness, as far from home as possible. And I was in this burning city, not knowing what my fate would be.

But my fate knew. She was only waiting to strike.

Seshadri never quite knew what to make of Partition. At one level, he knew that they had witnessed one of the most far-reaching changes in India's history and he was also astute enough to see that things would never go back to the way they had been before. He was irritated when some of the others talked of going back.

He had come upon one such conversation just a few days ago.

The fires had died down for the present, the mindless killings had stopped, Gandhiji had returned from Noakhali. The first wave of life-taking had passed over, leaving in its wake the flotsam and jetsam of another civilization, one that could not, it seemed, ever merge with the existing one, but had, in some cunning way, changed it, taking away its grace and innocence and leaving in its place the rawness and hardness of suffering and grief and waste.

It was Sen who was holding forth. They were having coffee in the canteen of the office.

'My wife does not like Calcutta,' he was saying. 'I think I will have to take her back to Dhaka.'

'Just wait for a few months,' someone else said. 'You can take her back then.'

Seshadri looked at them. He had just returned from Delhi. What he had seen there had been even more stark. Whole trains of people had been annihilated, chopped, and decimated. The survivors lived in refugee camps, ten or more to a tent, Kingsway had been made a steaming mess milling with people, India Gate was barely recognizable.

One evening he had decided to go to Old Delhi. He did not know why, for he was not in the least adventurous. In the evening sun, Jama Masjid stood silhouetted, breathtakingly lovely, the spires standing out like delicate tracery against the darkening sky.

Pigeons, unmindful of the destruction round them, flew in great swoops, arcing gracefully and settling back in the minarets.

There was something serious, almost grim, about the streets. The old tamarind trees, their leaves moving gently against the evening breeze remained the same, the roads beneath his feet were the same roads he had taken when, in what seemed a lifetime ago, but was only three years, he and Goutu and the children had gone to the Red Fort.

But it was not the same.

There was suspicion in the air, it hung like a pall. The very few people on the road were hurrying back home, almost all the shops were closed, although it was only six in the evening. There was something else, something Seshadri was aware of but could not quite place till much later.

Then it hit him—there had been no women and children on the streets.

'Do you really think your wife can go back,' he now asked.

'Yes, yes', said Sen excitedly. 'We have an old house, my uncle and his family are taking care of it till we return.'

'I think you will have to tell your wife to get used to Calcutta,' said Seshadri in that slow, deliberate way he had when he was making a pronouncement and did not think he could be contradicted, 'No one can go back to Pakistan, east, or west.' He got up, leaving Sen and the others to glare at his retreating back.

Later, Seshadri learnt that Sen's uncle had fled Dhaka for Calcutta when two of his sons had been butchered, in front of him, trying to save the house.

And so it was, my dears, that I did not get widowed then for my husband was saved. Then something happened that none of us could make sense of. Gandhiji was killed! His murderer was Nathuram Godse and he had been killed when going to his prayers. He had died saying He Ram!

So even Vishnu could not save Gandhiji.

We were all stuck to the radio. My father had come to see how things were and as a gift for the house, for he could not come empty-handed, he'd bought us a radio. After the way I had let him down and Achyut and his wife had separated and paati, his mother had died, there was nothing more for my father to do except sometimes write to me, but the letters had to be received in secret because my husband would not speak to my father. This meant a lot of lying because I had now to get my postcards myself, but, after all, my dears what is the point of life if everyone only wants the truth? The postman would come after he had left for office and I had to tear up his letters as soon as I read them. Posting my letters was the easy part because I would just hide them in my vegetable bag.

So the radio had been a present from him. My husband might not have spoken to my father, but did not mind taking his gifts. The first time he had come to Calcutta, he had gone from the station to a distant cousin's house. He visited us, radio in the rickshaw, and I opened the door. The girls were at school and I was alone in the house. My father had come visiting from Madras and no payasam even, to welcome him!

He stayed on till my husband returned and rose from his chair when he entered. Neither knew what to say. This was the first time they were meeting after that fateful, distant day when my father thanked him for his kindness in keeping me on as his wife. The scene was as clear as a mirror in my mind. No doubt they both were also thinking of it.

The awkwardness was like a brick wall. My father would not meet his eyes, and as for my husband he just went inside.

He had his dinner with us and then got up to leave. My husband was reading some thick book that the shelves were filled with.

Was my husband not going to say 'Let your father stay with us'?

So I said it. Yes, my dears, I told my father Appa you must stay here. You cannot go now in the night.

My husband threw the book he was reading, it fell to the floor with a sound like a gunshot. He went inside and lay down.

My father said in a worried whisper, 'I don't think Mapillai likes my staying. After all, you were not a good girl.'

Not a good girl? What did it mean, being a good girl? I had done, was still doing, everything I was expected to do. The house like a piece of glass, shining, the very floors reflecting the care I gave it. The children were beautifully turned out, my husband's clothes, right down to his socks were washed and smoothed out; no dears, I did not have an iron until later.

But even now, when I am sitting in this chair, almost half a century after it all happened, with husband, Achyut and Krishnanand all dead and gone and turned to ashes, I get the old feeling of anger rising like a red monster inside me, choking my throat and making speech impossible.

That day, I did not budge. I put a pai on the floor, set down a pillow and said 'Lie down here, Appa.'

I could hear the moans coming from the inner room and I could almost hear the girls, they were so silent. Let him moan. I was not going to bend. The strength of Khudida's mother and the women who had left their homes at Partition came into me.

My husband did not speak to me the next day and by the end of the third day, the girls were almost prostrate with anxiety.

'Please say sorry, ma,' the elder one begged.

I looked at both of them. Would I go back to Madras and start all over again like the women of the Partition?

No, I would not. I did not have their strength—yet.

So I started apologizing and cringing and by the end of the fourth day, we were back to normal. My father had left.

Now we were at our posts, near the radio. Yes, every historical event that happened then in the country, had a history to match in our house.

Nathuram Godse had killed Gandhiji, our Father, and Nehru spoke on the radio. He used a lot of big words, only my husband understood all that he said but we could hear the grief in his voice. We all cried and then there was the funeral. It was all on the radio.

India had become independent. The British had left. But not without blood. Very cleverly they had managed to make us take our own blood, through the Partition, through the killing of Hindus and Muslims by their own countrymen, through rape and violation and the killing of the Mahatma. Who said it was all ahimsa, dears? There was a lot of himsa, rakhtam, blood. We have seen it all.

Calcutta's patron saint, the River Ganga, flowed majestically along, the end of a journey begun in the highest reaches of the Himalayas, from its ice-bound, majestic, secretive sombre heights through the plains of northern India, everywhere worshipped as mother goddess, a living, breathing creature, symbolizing life—and death—to the millions living along her banks.

To Goutu, the river had become a metaphor of life. The Hooghly and its many moods, with its swirling waters, or its calm summer sheen, its grey wetness in the relentless downpours of Calcutta's monsoons, finally merging with winter's fogs in an indeterminate bluey-green, joining the sea at Ganganagar, its journey's end, reminding her of that other life-giving river where her own life had begun. But it had taken away life too, and from her place on the riverbank where they were all sitting after a trip to Dakshineshwar, she could see the sudden flares of funeral pyres before they settled down to a steady blaze that licked up the body and swallowed all that was the person and left only the ashes.

Many times she thought of the river near her childhood-home. No not her home but her childhood prison, where she had been beaten, starved and more than anything unloved and not understood for the spark of her personality, where her loves had been abruptly put out before they had to even flame and then burn to a steady glow. All of it was acrid, like smoke, sometimes choking her, darting here and there with unsteady movements, attaching itself to this person and that, to this object and that, changing like the colours of a chameleon, not filling her with joy, only filing her with an unspeakable sadness. Her aunts were alive, holding court in distant Madras, they had forgotten her, though she had not forgotten, only managed to push it all deep down from where it surfaced in occasional bursts of bright light, now reducing her, in her new found feeling of futility, gratified that someone thought her worthy of attention, however fleeting.

She thought back to Subra, turned the thought over briefly in her mind and put it back again.

The river flowing past her now had the power to move her, she had seen the book of maps her daughters now possessed and they had shown her the course of the river where she had spent the first few years of her married life and they had lived out their infancies. They had shown her the Yamuna, she knew it from Delhi and then again on a visit to Agra, flowing past the Taj Mahal. She had been struck with the grandeur of the Taj, when they had turned the corner and seen the minarets, gleaming in the moonlight like the pearly skin of a woman, that incandescent north Indian winter moon so different from the moon of her home. She remembered how her breath had almost stopped when she had seen it standing there, there had been so many people, everyone had been talking and there was lots of noise but a hush fell over all of them when the Taj loomed out, gleaming with a new beauty and renewed perfection, each time.

The Ganga, though, was different. Many of the shlokams of her childhood came back to her mind, the first lines of the *Ganga-sthotram*

Devi sureshwaribhagavathi gange tribhhuvanatarini taralatarange

Sankaramouli viharini vimale mama mathirasthamtava padakamale.

As she said it to herself, the realization that she was sublimating some of her desires, her body-awareness, into what she called bhakti: the wick-making, the scrubbing of her shrine had become more intense, it had become an end in itself.

Seshadri had long stopped watching her at these jobs and the girls, too, had become serious about their studies. The elder one would be a lawyer, the younger wanted to be a teacher. She had become unimportant to their lives and it was galling to her that the taking down of the violin from its place in the shelf no longer signalled their hour of togetherness, when the girls looked on admiringly and with such love at her fingers flying up and down on the strings, the bow drawn back and forth in perfect time. The last time, the elder one had actually left the room, she had to do her homework!

'Come back here!' she had ordered.

'I have to do my homework,' she had answered, almost defiantly.

Goutu rushed up to her, with a fearful look on her face. Were the children going to leave her? She would not let them. She would keep them by her side, forever. She had lost her sister to death, her brother to life—and Krishnanand? She did not know to what.

No. The children would not be allowed to leave her.

'How dare you!' she screamed. 'Leave the house!'

'Oh, all right,' said the girl. She opened the door and left. Her younger sister came out.

''Don't, don't' she said, her breath coming out in gasps. She hated unpleasantness.

But the child had already left, down a little side road on to the main road that would in five minutes come to the market.

Goutu had the humiliating task of running behind her and bringing her back.

Once inside, all hell broke loose. It was as if the combined bitterness of the aunts and the loveless marriage had broken the dam and was spilling over the banks, drowning reason, submerging sanity. She beat the girl until her own hand hurt and it was as if she did not hear the child shouting in fear and pain and humiliation.

Later she felt ashamed. She looked at the child's swollen face and her bruises and she averted her eyes. Then after a few days, peace was made, but things never went back to being the same again.

No one recognized, least of all Goutu herself that a new Goutami was struggling to take birth, a Goutami who would do away with pretence, with family pressure, with compliance to society's norms. Her loneliness hit her afresh. She had no one to talk to, no one to get advice from. She did not care for the advice she did get—they were merely instructions. Sometimes she looked at her friends: Manorama, Tulasi, Binidini, Mangalam. They all had mothers they could go back to. She was aware of the strange looks they sometimes gave her when she was saying things no one would, making comments, being pushy. Why didn't one of them say 'You shouldn't have said that.' Or 'You can do it like this'? They just looked away and later avoided her.

As for her cousins, she had lost touch with all of them. The letters, at first desultory, had by now dried up. She had written but when no one replied she too had given up. Who cared anyway?

She did, though she pretended she didn't.

She got up from the seat and they went back home. The children were tired and Seshadri was now really important in his place of work and his face wore that distant look it assumed when thinking of office. She did not care to lighten the mood in the boat going across.

They got off at the bus stop and Seshadri said they would take a rickshaw home.

Her Bengali was better than his for she was an adept at languages but today she would not join in the spirited bargaining that was going on. Let him shout and make Tamil noises and gestures, she would just get on and sit if she were told to. The children looked up at her. Was she ill? This was a new side to Amma, keeping silent instead of jumping into the fray.

Eventually they got in and the rickshaw set off. They came past lake Market and into the side road and the house inside the paara appeared. It was a large rambling place and housed a number of families in its different parts. As usual, their neighbour Bolai, a Rabindra Sangeet exponent, who claimed he had gone to Shantiniketan and had been taught by the Gurudev himself, was practising. The words of the song, accompanied by the harmonium wafted back to them:

Kano chokher jole bhijiye dilem na?

Shukhno dhulo joto.....

Someone, perhaps a friend of Bolai's was sitting on the cement chair in front of their door, She could see a lit cigarette glowing in the dark... She got off and the children, half-asleep, staggered in with her.

She did not even glance at the man sitting there. She turned the key in the lock and was about to go in.

'Goutu,' said a voice, deep and well-remembered.

She stopped as if paralysed, the key half-turned in the lock. It was a voice that would wake her from the dead, such was the power it had.

She turned round slowly, the girls by now fully awake. Seshadri was walking towards them.

'Krishnanand,' she said. Happiness was flooding her. So she was not dead after all! She was alive, she felt young again, every pore and cell in her body was functioning, her joy in life had not been doused out.

He was alive and kicking, this cousin of hers the one who had the power to make her feel like a woman, like a human being.

He was smiling that old half-smile, delicious, langorous. The heavy-lidded eyes had lost none of their power to mesmerise her and she didn't care who saw.

She held out her hand and he took it in both of his. The years fell away and they were back in Madurai to that old house of memories and they had just finished that tantalising kiss, with grandfather just inside the door.

Seshadri was standing beside them. Their faces were rapturous, his own—inscrutable. He knew there were going to be some changes in his life, again.

But even he could not have known how much. That was yet to come. The energies of the earth, the shakti which sends breezes into motion, which sways trees and fells them, and creates waves which lash the shores, were drawing their strength into themselves so that the storm that was going to change their lives would redouble its force.

There is nothing I can say, my dears, about that moment when I realized that it was Krishna sitting in that chair, that cement chair that I thought was so ugly.

This happiness was complete, it made me whole, not cut up into parts so that I had to be different to different people.

When I had my hand in his, my heart was in the hand I gave him. Who cared for what he felt? I felt all these things and I knew that I was not the woman who had been afraid, afraid of asking her father to stay in her house, of going out, of spending fifteen rupees on buying a sari, of visiting a friend who was having an illicit love affair, of having to write out all the expenses for the day making sure I had the money I was supposed to have to the last pie.

No—I was meant for more than this and I was going to get it. This talk of duty and virtue and goodness and respect—what were they but words that I too repeated to be accepted by my friends?

You know dears, these are only words, now that I am sitting here and waiting for Yama, I can tell you that they only become real when you have been shown love and respect and duty.

I had felt love for my paati because she had given me love.

I had some feelings of duty for my father because he had fulfilled some of his responsibilities. I know something about virtue because, yes, my husband was virtuous. He had not let us all down when he could have.

But I had not found it all in one person. And not always.

Krishna and I were together in this friendless world, trying to make what sense we could of the madness called life. Some of the blood that coursed through our veins was the same. We had been sent away, exiled, no one wanted us both for we reminded them of unpleasant and uncomfortable things of the long-ago and the far away that they would rather forget.

No one ever needed to think of us as long as we were banished like this to the far flung corners of the strife-torn new India They could wear their silk saris and malli-poo in their oiled, black hair and attend kutcheries in the sabhas.

They could sit in their thinnais and swing lazily on their wooden oonjals and play pallankuzhi and shout with joy as steaming cups of coffee were brought out to them. They could go for six months at a time for delivery and be massaged and bathed and dried with the fragrant smoke of the samrani.

The men could go to the beach and watch the first show on the first day of a movie's release and sit together on the benches and exchange news.

Yes—both of us had been forgotten. We were making our own lives in this corner of the country, or that.

And so it is that the river of life flows on and takes with her any pieces of wood or straw that lie on her banks, the little pieces that have somehow been forced to break away. Krishna and I would now share a common fate, we would be bound together.

And that is the way it was.

Seshadri had never felt as fatalistic as he did now. He thought of the first line of the letter he had written to Narayanan when Goutu had gone off the rails—he called it The Affair to himself—and he thought about it often.

Yes, he had written a letter. There was a copy in a file marked Goutami and it was stored in the Yellow Box, which his daughters were sternly told never to touch. In the file were also the anonymous letters he had got, informing him about the Subra business.

Dear father-in-law, he had written. The skies have fallen on us, but with the grace of Venkatachalapathy, we shall somehow get through. I want you to come here as soon as you can....

He had not been exaggerating. The skies had indeed fallen for him. For, unbeknownst to Goutami, Seshadri had fallen madly—for him—in love with Goutu. It had burned like a steady flame and he had not faltered even once in this feeling. He thought her beautiful, accomplished, talented and her cooking and housekeeping had found their way to his heart.

It was her total lack of logic that was the only difficulty—that and her lying. Once she got over these two things—and Seshadri believed that by constant application she could—she would be like himself, perfect.

Seshadri believed that he was the perfect example of the realized atman and, in these last five years, decided that he had perfected the art of detachment as expounded in the Gita.

Watching Goutu light the lamp in the shrine one day, eyes shut, palms folded in complete silence as she did her namaskarams, he had said, lightly, 'Why don't you do namaskarams to me instead? It would be as efficacious.' It was said only half in jest. He would have accepted her namaskarams with perfect ease if she had taken him at his word.

She had not. She had said with some spirit 'Only God deserves our namaskarams,' and tried to take the edge off by laughing.

He had not spoken to her for a few hours, but being a just man, realized at least the intellectual falsity of his words. The girls always did nmaskarmas to him before their exams. No one ever knew what he was thinking as they bent down in front of him.

That night, as he lay there with the children and Goutu by his side, he tried to think in a logical way. He went down one train of thought, then another, one syllogism, then another but for once, found that there were some things that defied the law of gravity or any other law he could think of.

He had seen the look, the current, passing through them at the moment of their meeting. She was illumined by the strength of her own feelings, he saw that. She had not even waited to see what he would say. She had just added another plate on the verandah floor, where they all sat in a line to eat and she put down a pai and a bed and a pillow for Krishna to lie down on.

What must he do? Stand by and watch the drama unfold? Take recourse in his own work and leave the rest to fate? Send her back to her father this time, if anything untoward happened? He decided that the last course of action was the best. He turned over and lay quietly on his side, too unhappy even to moan. But he did not sleep.

The next morning he got up and found to his relief that Krishnanand was still asleep in the front room. He could hear the sounds from the kitchen so he, too, made his usual getting-up sounds, the belching, the noisy turning off of the fan, the squelching while he spat out the toothpaste...

When he went into the kitchen, she had the coffee ready exactly as he liked it—the taste, the temperature, the colour...

He looked at her back. The one plait had been replaced by a bun, khopa as she had been taught to call it. She did not go in search of flowers to put in her hair any more. Good, it had been an unnecessary extravagance. She was still very slim, must be all that housework she did as one possessed, house-proud as she was. She wore only silk saris, they were sent from Madras by Narayanan, now in his seventieth year. Narayanan had no one else in his life now, a brief and disastrous reconciliation with Achyut had been unsuccessfully attempted. Achyut had come home drunk every night in succession for two weeks and hurled accusations at Narayanan. It had been these that Narayanan had found difficult to swallow and so, in the end, he had been forced to tell him to leave.

Seshadri found himself ruminating on the many things that he had been forced to accept—the black hair colouring now used more extensively, the different kinds of dishes that appeared at mealtimes instead of his favourites, the bureau of the two keys that had come with them, if a trifle worn, across the plains of north India, hiding more and more things from open view, the children speaking Bengali at home instead of chaste Tamil, reading Bankim Chandra Chatterjee and Sarath Chandra and Tagore rather than the Thirukkural and Bharathiar.... She herself had a reading list he did not approve of. They were all love stories set in England, though he had told her to read only Charles Dickens and Walter Scott.

Yes she was a rebel. It was impossible to fathom her, futile to try and bring her to heel.

The trouble was, he could not let her out of his life, or imagine one without her. She must never guess this or she would lose even the little fear she had for him. It was silly to admit these things, women took advantage of male weaknesses.

'How long is he going to stay?' he asked.

'Who?' she said, as if she didn't understand.

'Your cousin!'

The words were like stones being thrown at a glass pane. Let it shatter, she didn't care.

'I don't know. Let him get up,' she replied.

Krishna must get up before he, Seshadri, left, or anything may happen. Fortunately, Krishna got up and after his morning ablutions came to the kitchen door.

'Good morning,' he said, in that conversational way he had. It always set Seshadri's teeth on edge.

Seshadri did not reply. This was a greeting reserved for the office, ridiculous to say it one's own home he thought.

Goutu had made his coffee and she gave it to him. Both looked quite normal but the way Goutami turned around once or twice did not augur well.

More sounds reached his ears. The girls had got up and were having their usual arguments, whispering furiously. Seshadri walked up to them before war actually broke out. His elder daughter thought she was already a lawyer, her speech had taken on the tone of judgments being delivered. Secretly, he was very proud of her—she had turned out to be practical and organized. He found her an able companion and he liked her logical way of arguing.

The other one was still a trifle timid, but she could be trained. To Seshadri, training was everything. He did not allow for swabhavam, a person's nature.

As Seshadri finished his coffee and Goutu took his tumbler to the kitchen, he found Krishnanand standing before him.

'When are you leaving for office, SKS?' he asked. He had taken to calling Seshadri by his initials. 'I'll leave with you. I have some work.'

So when Seshadri left for work, Krishnanand in tow, he thought his handling of the situation had been astute and absolutely faultless.

He could not have known that after Krishnanad finished his work, he had gone to the Grand Hotel, drunk himself silly, had come home, thrown up and had to be put to bed, where he lay, pretending to have a fever.

When the children came home, they found everything in order, with Amma at her usual post in the kitchen, so they could rush out of the house to play.

The first day had passed off uneventfully.

Yes, it had. I can't think of anything we did which was wrong. Though mind you, it's now over forty years since that fateful day. My husband wanted to know when he was going to leave and I said I thought in two days' time. He was now in Jabalpur, his wife and he had separated almost as soon as we had left for Delhi.

I did not ask why. I only asked if he had another wife, he said no.

'I am not made for marriage,' he said, 'Achyutan and I—we are the same.'

But Achyutan had four children! Foolish fellow, said Krishnanand.

It was unbelievable to have him in the same house, under the same roof, breathing the same air as I. This was what it meant to belong, to be normal, to be in the company of one who had the same beginning. When I mentioned Narayani or Valli, he could nod with understanding; I did not have to talk about them, to explain.

As I sat next to him, I felt as I had not felt since I had lain next to paati, safe, loved, looked after. I did not have to pay for the care with demands, with my body, with cooking, washing with the constant fear of being corrected or questioned.

The bitch of the diamond ear-rings and silks had expected gratitude and obedience. My husband expected service and obedience. Not much difference there!

I looked at him, afresh, some of his magnificence had diminished. His hair, now thinner and greyer did not sit quite so well on his head. Was there a slight paunch?

But I, too, had become older. Two children and discontent and an ache in my heart had made me different. My hands were rougher, my voice, my great charm, had become harsh. I hid my hands in my sari and curled my chapped feet into my petticoat.

No, the great pull had gone. But it had been replaced by something even stronger: an implacable desire not to lose the old days, to keep this man in my life forever, had taken over my mind.

That is what I was going to do. No one would stop me.

Krishnanand went back that time but work brought him to Calcutta again and again and it became understood that he would stay with SKS and Goutu. When he was in the house, she felt more alive, more vital, full of an energy that made her vibrant. The children liked his laughter, very much in short supply in their brief lives, serious and combative as they had been. They liked, too, that he brought little gifts for them, books with lovely pictures, chocolates, colouring pencils, things some of their friends had. Only, Goutu locked everything in the bureau. She was more possessive about the things than the children were and of course they had to be out of Seshadri's sight unless it was a birthday. Getting and unbirthday gift was profligacy of the worst kind....

So it was that by his fourth visit, both the girls' favourite person in the world was Amma's cousin, Krishna Mama. He could do no wrong in their eyes and the girls waited for him with Goutu's anticipation.

Now that he was back in her life, her love life with Seshadri took on a new colour. She simply imagined that it was Krishna she was making love to, the Krishna who understood her better than anyone else. Thinking about sleeping with Krishna and actually sleeping with him became the same thing, so she really did not know the difference. He made her life sweeter.

And so it was that, after many years, she found herself pregnant again. When she discovered this, the first shock was replaced by contentment. She thought she had achieved her ambition—of merging the past with the present.

It's surely not true, thought Seshadri. We can't afford another baby.

He told her as much. 'We have two daughters. How can we have another baby?'

She said she knew all that. She said she knew that they had to get them married....

He stopped her then and there.

'Not marriage,' he said. 'I don't like marriage. They must be made to study and work. They must study as much as they want to and they must be self-reliant. Marriage is the way women trap men into taking over their responsibilities.'

She couldn't sleep that night. It was she who had felt trapped, in a prison, and he was saying these things! She thought of the rules and regulations he had imposed on her in the last eighteen years and how she had battled to stay her own woman! She thought of Narayani, Mangala, Sudha. She thought briefly of Subra's sister.

She thought of herself. All of us had been married before our sixteenth birthday and had motherhood visited upon us by the time we were seventeen!

All right, let them not marry. In a way it is good, she thought, they would be with her in her old age, acting as a buffer between the two of them. And now she would add a third child to this.

Seshadri felt defeated. He had lost. Life was taking turns he had not factored in. The latest, the baby, was an unwelcome addition to his deliberate scheme of things. He thought briefly of his very successful career. He was now a force to be reckoned with, he had got noticed. His trips to Delhi were becoming more frequent and he knew there was going to be a move soon. He had not told Goutu this because she had a way of talking tactlessly and too much.

Well, he'd go ahead with his plans to send the girls to school and college in Madras. He hadn't mentioned this to Goutu yet, but he would—soon. He had come to realize that his work was soon going to mean many changes and the children must not be disturbed. In a year, the elder one would be ready for college and the younger girl was already in high school.

They would go to Madras and stay in hostels. They must be trained and it was better to remove them from Goutu's overpowering influence. As it was, he could see how strong was her hold on them, their minds and hearts. He didn't want their intellects to be taken over by her, that would be ruinous.

His own fine intellect did not make him realize that no power on earth would ever wipe Goutu out from their lives. She had coloured them different from the moment of their conception. Not for them the usual lines of thought, the common reactions: their sense of self had been nurtured by her very presence. Her intuitive gravitation toward the beautiful, the unreal, the imaginary, what he referred to as her 'dishonesty and lies', had added sparking dimensions to their lives.

He could send them away and he did. He was now powerful enough to influence decisions and the girls got in easily enough.

So bewildered and weeping, they went from their home, each taking with her that part she loved the most, wondering why they were being banished,

And Goutu? Their exile served only to tighten the screws of her resolve.

2

When Goutu told Seshadri that they were going to have another baby, Seshadri felt defeated. Goutu's genius for ambushing his plans made him feel violent. And in the course of the nine months that it takes to bring a human being into this world, Seshadri did become violent.

He hated the idea of having another child. The girls were both nearly adults and the desire to go through the natural stages of fatherhood had completely left him. He was in his mid-forties and this new development suddenly changed his life plans for himself, for them all.

But he didn't know how much all of it was going to change, to what extremes it was going to take them all. If he had, he may have done what he stopped himself from doing when he had caught her with Subra, sent her home to her father. For, really speaking, they had moved away from each other, this affair of the baby and her obtuseness proved that.

Many times in the first few weeks when she had dropped the bombshell of the baby, he had tried. At first, reasoning, then arguing and, finally, using violence. He had told her their financial situation did not allow it, talked about the increasing fees of the two girls that had to be paid. He knew that it was all in vain. She did not understand.

He watched her now, as he had done before in these twenty years, going about her housework. No more flowers, no fineries. He believed though that the black in her hair came out of a bottle. The black lipstick case had been abandoned and in its place had come a better thing, which in her lexicon, meant something more expensive.

This was the thing that he found most difficult to understand—her total disregard for the family as a social unit. He went over this many times in his mind; at forty five, Seshadri's mind was like a rapier, age had given it greater sharpness, but it remained without the shine of understanding. Whatever did not follow rules was outside his range of truth and must be cut off with the sword of discrimination, the mind.

So he did not know what to do. Several questions remained unanswered. Did she not see how all of them would be plunged into chaos? That it was a retrograde step?

The girls were embarrassed, the elder one thought—and it was apparent from the way she looked at them—that it was shameful that they were having sex when they were so old. Neither disclosed the fact of their mother's pregnancy to any of their friends. Did they want a son? Was that why this was happening?

Actually neither Seshadri nor Goutu thought of this. Goutu did not see what good Achyut's presence had done in her father's life and she didn't think Krishna was a particularly dutiful son either. Nor, for that matter, had Seshadri been. His father had died only the previous year and they had done nothing more than being present at the ceremonies, conducted on the banks of the river that flowed past their village home. Goutu thought briefly of her father's presence at the ceremonies. Narayanan, now bent with the burden of the many tricks life had played upon him, had dutifully arrived with a ring in a velvet box for his son-in-law. That ring was to grace the hand that had lit the funeral pyre. It had nine stones, neatly arranged in a square setting, each stone signifying a planet and begging it to be kind, to show its benevolent face to the wearer. Goutu had taken a look at it.

'Why did you bring this?' she had asked

Narayanan had said nothing at first, just gazed at her with his half smile. Goutu saw with a pang his grey hair, even his eyebrows were grey. He has become very old, she thought and her mind went back to that distant day in the past when he had pleaded with her husband to keep a motherless child. The scene was graven in her memory.

As it was in his. She understood that the minute she repeated her question.

'There was no need for you to do this,' she said. 'He doesn't expect such things.'

'You were a bad girl,' answered her father. 'He could have sent you away.'

Goutu turned away, but not before the memory of the scene had gone through her heart like an arrow, sharp as an arrow too the words that Subra had spoken 'A man's got to live, hasn't he?'

That evening, when all the others were sitting in the central koodam, she had sat in the shadows of the room, where nobody could see her face. A thousand thoughts were passing through her mind. She went through the twenty years of their marriage, of the distant Himalayan capital, so far from home, of herself, of Seshadri, of Sridevi—funny, she hadn't thought of her for a long time. Only one thing stood out, like a constant thread, a backdrop, a basic ragam, play it how you will, and that was Krishnanand.

In the last few months, she had told him first haltingly, then in a rush, about Subra. When she looked up, his expression was inscrutable.

'Do you think of me as a bad girl?' she had asked in Tamil.

'No, only human,' he had answered and it had been as if a great weight had been lifted off her shoulders. His face had been inscrutable. That expression, full of a fearsome quality which

Achyut had learnt to recognize many many years ago, came back to shutter his face.

Now sitting in this large hall, resembling the waiting room in a wayside station, with everyone in Seshadri's family only like travelling companions, she turned over these words in her heart. Good, bad. Right, wrong. Clever, stupid.

What about people like her and Krishna who were not good, but not bad either? They did wrong things, but they were also right, weren't they? What was Seshadri's cleverness if it didn't give him understanding?

Subra had been bad. He had repaid her innocence with intrigue. So why did her father think she had been bad? She was looking for something, did he not see that? Krishnanand was also looking for the same thing. They were together in this search.

Thirteen days later, they took the train back to Calcutta. Seshadri's father's mortal remains were in an urn to be submerged where the Ganga meets the sea. Seshadri was fulfilling his filial duties even if his father had been irresponsible. His mother had wailed loudly when he had gone to take leave of her. Seshadri's face mirrored his surprise, she had always been so taciturn. Her words when he could understand them, surprised him even more.

'He has left me for ever,' she said, 'but when was he ever there?'

Seshadri said nothing. He was a loyal son.

Yes dears, now that I am sitting here, on my own except for her, I can understand what my mother-in-law said.

But then, at that time, my father's words only made me more resolute in my decision to make sure that my life and Krishnanand's remained intertwined. We had been like two rivers, flowing side by side, now rough, now smooth, now broad, now narrow, now dry, now in flood, now with people, now without. These two rivers would have to join. It was a duty I had to myself.

The doorbell rings. There is a clang of the bangle on the metal rim of her chair and she opens the door. It is a visitor. Our darkness is going to be lit up by a visitor. But only for a short while, then back we go to our lonely lives, she and I. We are both beside ourselves with joy and babble on like kettles on the boil. What do we say? Not much. No one wants to hear it.

But when I got pregnant, my husband tried to dissuade me from having the baby. My mind was made up. This was going to come to fruit, this fight for recognition, the struggle for love. I did not know then that the only kind of love that was worth struggling for comes from within. I have learnt it too late.

Which is the life well-lived? The one which like my husband's he strove to plan, or mine, which just took each situation as the only one? Now that he is gone, I can look back and wonder at the passing of the wheel of time which renders all things meaningless. I didn't have to do anything, it has all slipped away into nothingness, these eighty odd years, beginning with that day when my mother gave birth, my mother who I didn't even know, but whose absence proved to be a stronger influence on my life than her presence might have been.

I wonder now, if I had sought her face in the face of that aunt of diamonds and silk, whether Achyut had looked for her in that Chitti of ours and never found her. And what about my father?

What about Krishna and all his women? Who were they?

It all lies inside of us, locked away. A small part of this and a small past of that. We just make gestures of wholeness. Purnam idam, purnam adam....

Seshadri and Goutu came back and then this! No one would have thought that this would be the latest offering!

Seshadri thought of his own mother, who had, he counted, no less than ten children, although only five now remained. In the train, he had had enough time to ponder her words, her parting shot to him. So all the time she had been angry with his father for being away and coming back only to get her pregnant! He had thought of her as patient and all-absorbent. It had been locked away, she had not told anyone of her resentment. He thought of her struggles in their village home, he was surprised at the intensity and clarity of his remembering. He had not forgotten anything either—the poverty, the deprivations, the insults. He thought again of the first time he had left home to go to college, almost the first person in his village to go so far for post-graduate studies. She had had to sell her remaining gold bangle. He had never thought of getting her another one, why hadn't he? She had been in the smoky kitchen, he had come in with the letter in his hand and looked at her. She had looked at him. There were not too many words exchanged. She had wordlessly slipped off her bangle and he had taken it and left the room. Even when he left his home some days later, knowing that he would never come back to live there, she had watched him go.

He had cut his hair and taken off his earrings many years ago. His grandfather had been disapproving but being taciturn was a family trait. And so other people's thoughts, viewpoints, objections had never found their way into the open. After this beginning, to be married to Goutu had been both a challenge and an irritant. Challenge because he was required to come up with responses alien to him, irritating because he could never make her understand that a wife must walk seven steps behind her husband, in every way. He thought, uncharacteristically for him, of the day the infamous steel bureau had come into the house. Rightfully he should have been asked for permission and his things should have found pride of place inside.

By the end of the two day journey, Seshadri had worked himself up to a fine passion of justifiable rage. No one could have dared tell him that it was the grief of losing a stranger who had sired him that was making him so angry. He shared his mother's anger and misery but pairs of opposites—right wrong, good bad—were holding him prisoner.

Reaching their home, Goutu rushed for the broom and wiping cloths as the only objects that made life recognizable. She had made cleanliness one of the objectives of her life, you could clean a table or shine the floor even if you couldn't quite clean your mind or acknowledge some thoughts.

Her thoughts went to Krishna. Was this love? She had read enough to know that there was a thing called love for which empires had been lost and gained.

Was the steady loyalty shown by Seshadri love? Did love take many forms, wear different veshams, disguises, like the therukoothu dancers who played many parts? She couldn't decide. Because Goutu did not know to use her mind, her heart was where she made her decisions and of course her heart, not a very reliable thing, made her fickle.

Seshadri went to office and that weekend they took a boat from under the Hooghly bridge and Goutu and Sesahdri, with Goutu holding on to the side of the boat, made their way to the middle of the Ganga, where Seshadri lowered the mud pot containing his father's mortal remains, some ashes and a few pieces of bone, into the dark mysterious breast of Bhishma-janani to be carried into the sea, completely at one with the elements.

Then he went back to his work the next day, and turned his mind to other things. He could concentrate on his work, he hoped, no more disturbances.

In that he was wrong.

Well dears. I think you feel my memory is very good. No, there my husband was better than me, but my memory for my feelings is sharp and clear. I can recall what I felt.

I can tell you if you care to listen, though now there are not many people who want to do that. When I phone my daughters, they only want me to put the phone down. Then my thoughts go back to those days when they sat around me to listen to the music I could make, though now my fingers are too twisted to fly up and down the violin.

Going to the village home stirred up something in my mind. Dark, muddied water now entered my mind and I went back to the days of thirty-odd years ago when I was part of another home which taught me nothing but violence and self-defence and lying. The journey has been a misery of feelings, opposing and emotional, nothing made sense any more. I thought back to the many rivers that had nurtured me and the goddesses of those rivers.

Do you know what I think of river goddesses? They control the rivers themselves, the river is their home and when the angry waters rise, sometimes submerging the abode of those goddesses, there is an exchange within the swirling waters, the waters rush in to the devi and she, even though she seems to be standing still in impassive observation, actually welcomes these waters as one would a favourite child. Then later, after the waters have receded, she emerges with renewed energy and strength, to face her devotees who have worshipped her for centuries

The time has come for me to allow these waters to enter my mind and life, to get submerged and start afresh, but not before I had come to understand what the absence of a home has been, what it had meant to never have a place where I was enveloped in understanding. I thought of my father, he had grown old with bitterness, in the recent meeting I had asked about Achyutan, and received a blank stare in reply. So he was wifeless and sonless, and my husband had made his daughter out of bounds too.

Where was Achyutan? He had moved from Delhi, had given up his job with the paper he had been working for, had made a mess of his marriage, just as his marriage had made a mess of him and his beautiful wife had left with the children. He had been seen in Madras, he had also been seen in Bombay, Krishnanand had said very briefly that he was not in touch. Of course my husband could never allow him to cross our door.

I ran through my mind with the list of cousins who had brought us to this. Narayani had become a grandmother. We had met and I had felt a great happiness at sitting with her. Who says not having a family sets you free? Then Valli. She had become fatter with middle age and as for the others, they had all met life half-way and allowed things to wash over them, riding the waves. Was I the only one then who had got submerged? Then like the goddess of the rivers, had I come out with greater strength and vitality?

There are no real answers to these questions. But my life provided the answers which I had to understand as we all do my dears, through truth or lies, whatever you will. In life, even my lies have sometimes provided the answers.

Seshadri

Seshadri's mind was playing tricks, yes it was. He was furious with himself, with Goutu, with the girls, with circumstances. For one thing, it was bent on going back into the past and doing a search. His mother's parting words were a transgression of trust. They were taking him back to a place which had remained uninhabited for over forty years. Into this desert place he had been thrust, no one had asked him permission, his thinking, up to now like a river flowing to its natural end, the sea, was now being met by other rivers and creating little whirlpools of confusion and the result was unexpected.

He was being made to go by these rogue thoughts, these disturbing little tributaries, to face the past, which according to him was inaccessible by its pastness. For to Seshadri, the past had gone and the future might never come, so the present was all that mattered. This thought had given him a lot of pride—he had come to believe that in his person was conflated the essence of the Upanishads, the non-duality of being and the illusory nature of life. It was all a dream, so to his horror, yes horror, why were the old scenes being replayed so vividly in his mind, and that other place which actually had the power to ache: the heart?

However it was, Seshadri was forced to watch another thing which he had eschewed, that strange, curious word, but one which described it perfectly, a movie, only this time he could not, by his stern looks and grim silences, foreboding evil for anyone who disobeyed, turn it off. For it was playing in his own head and try as he might, he could not walk away from his own head.

So it was that he was being forced to see a small boy in a single veshti, with poonool and tuft, complete with earrings, walking towards the village temple, brothers in tow, carrying a vessel which would be filled with the prasadam of the day, taking this back to his house. He had cringed with humiliation when he met anyone on the road, they were all his relatives, some of them very rich but no one really who cared. Then he would go back, his mother would be waiting, silent, with the other children in the house and they would eat this in that soot-filled house, with a narrow stairway leading to the top of the house.

The humiliation had soon congealed into anger when he discovered that his father, on his occasional sightings, actually impregnated his mother and then after a few weeks left for the next destination, wherever it was.

They must be made to pay for it. He would leave as soon as was possible, he had realized that the only way was to make sure he used his brain, a powerful tool, and stopped the thing called heart, with all its little fanciful beatings and imaginings, from telling him what to do.

He recalled an incident thought to be dead and interred.

It was his grandfather, who had taken charge of them all when his son, the recalcitrant husband and father, had turned out to be one whose lust for his wife's body was only equalled by his wanderlust.

There was, in one corner of the old village home, a palanquin. It was part of the bride price paid for this self-same grandfather, when as a mere stripling of thirteen, he had gone to the neighbouring village to be married. He had wanted a palanquin in much the same way as a boy might want a cricket bat, and had refused to tie the thaali until this whim had been satisfied. Despite this incongruous start, he had turned out to be their mainstay, and he remembered how he had to run up to the nearest town, a good five miles away, to fetch him his English paper so that he could read about Gandhiji.

'I am not going today,' he had said, once.

His grandfather had looked at him. His look held such contempt that Seshadri had left without a word.

So there was a price to be paid for a roof over one's head. At that precise moment, as it were—if one could actually time the actual second when momentous decisions are made—Seshadri had decided what his next course of action should be. He must leave the village and embark on the great journey alone, he must lock up the weakness of attachment and in a disengaged manner occupy himself with the business of doing well for himself.

None of his brothers or sisters must matter, he must realize that they were all fellow travellers on the journey and he may or may not see them again, his parents were the two entities who had placed him on life's path, into which he had made an appearance through his mother's womb, and he must understand this.

So without any scenes of the despair of parting, so essential to Goutu's nature, he had cut his hair, divested himself of the kadakans, the earrings, but not of the poonool, he still wore it, it was his tribute to his beginnings, and held no other import.

He saw too, in these fantastic re-runs of the past, the boy he had been, the slavery of poverty, the migration to a larger city and then, finally when his education had been completed to his own satisfaction, because Seshadri had developed very stringent standards for himself, he allowed himself the thrill of realizing that yes, it had indeed been a brilliant academic career, he had made his way to that seat of governmental power, Delhi, thousands of miles from his beginnings, putting as much distance as he could between all that it stood for and his present ambitions. He had successfully resisted any attempts to go back to his former sentimental state over his village home, though he had to admit that this had been difficult. His mother had come within the range of his mind's eye with disturbing regularity.

As he sat in his car and was being driven to work, he thought that yes, he had reached that state of grandeur when it had been decided that his mind could not be cluttered with thoughts of whether to turn right or left at the roundabouts, he thought of the way his life had played out.

I did it well, thought Seshadri to himself, I who walked several miles to school, crossed swollen rivers to get to my goal, who pushed a bicycle in the crags of the Himalayas, who took buses through the strife-torn, partition-riven streets of Calcutta, I have attained to the stature of greatness and power. But what about my home? Goutu filled me with a certain longing and happiness and I did my best with her, but she couldn't and still can't look at truth and accept what is staring her in the face. He thought of his sisters, the one who had been accused of having no sex organs, but who now had three children, thereby proving her mother-in-law a liar, as well as another who had married and gone away to some distant destination. He had visited her on his travels, now made comfortable while she, married to one of his own village cousins, had not been able to keep pace. Neither of them ever lied. They looked at things as they were and described them in simple, unstylised terms.

Then why had it, thought Seshadri, fallen to his lot to marry a woman who had such a powerful imagination that she only thought in terms of what a thing might be rather than what it actually was? Why had she ruined all of them with that flagrant departure from the path of right thinking with Subra? Seshadri felt his bile rising at the very thought. After all these years, he still wondered if he had done the right thing. He had done what he wanted to do, he had wanted her presence in his life and he had not exercised his intelligence.

But the girls could not be without a mother, he had to think of that. Yes, he had done the right thing, he had thought of the girls.

And yes, the girls had certainly been brought up with flair, he could see the difference in their appearance. Only they were both as much creatures of their own inner longings and irrational judgements as their mother. With grumpy satisfaction he had to acknowledge that the violin sessions had stopped, reduced first by the schoolwork and a few months ago, by their departure to Madras to study.

The car stopped and Seshadri was jerked out of his reverie by the sharp braking which flung him slightly forward in his seat. He resisted the temptation to tell his driver how to slow down, two men, sashed and turbanned, were now rushing forward, one to hold the door open, another to carry his bag and his lunch. Seshadri never ate out, he felt it would make him dull and over-burden his digestion and of course Goutu must not be given too much free time. She liked packing his lunch, there were lots of little boxes, each containing a different item of food, wheels within wheels, rather like her own mind, all colourfully arranged.

He went into his room. One of the three phones on his large, glass-topped tables rang.

He lifted the receiver. 'Seshadri here,' he said, speaking with a pronounced Tamil accent, partly deliberately chosen. Seshadri was not going to change in any way. Let them know this.

Whoever was on the other side started off. Seshadri did not speak Hindi unless the other person did not know English. It was his way of telling the world about Tamil and Tamilians. He answered in his precise way, weighing each word before he uttered it, as if letting go of an astram, which once it leaves the hand of the user, can never be used again.

His movie must be put on hold now, though somewhere in the darkening theatre, he saw the silhouette of a wife who was beginning to show that she was pregnant.

Pregnant she certainly was. Goutu had not told Seshadri, but the child was making its presence felt with tentative kicks, gentle, and feeble. Goutu felt excited. It would be good to have this baby, a part of a distant past that she was not going to leave behind, of making sure that she had someone who would listen to the violin when she wanted it to. For to Goutu's immense grief, the girls had been sent away to Madras to study.

Sehsadri had done it all on his own. She had not suspected a thing, she did not know that they were going to be so rudely torn away from the house, nor that she herself would feel so bereft when they left. She had stood stunned and of course, it had been a letter which had brought the news.

Goutu remembered all the letters in her life which had made change imminent. The first had been the one which she herself had so long ago written and posted to Krishnanand, begging him to come and rescue her. She sat up with a start. Had he ever received it? She would ask him if they ever met again.

Then, the one from her father which had fluttered at her like a leaf, Seshadri saying that he must never come to the house again. She knew that to be the day when she had lost her fear of consequence, she did not care from that moment what might happen.

Then she thought of that paralyzing day when Seshadri had appeared as she was with Subra, letter in hand and her whole world had changed in those few minutes. Yes it had. In the space of those few days between being discovered and her father's arrival, Goutu had seen apparitions of fear and abandonment and rejection that she scarcely could give name to.

Why was it so arranged that you had to conform to a certain pattern before you could be accepted into the fold? Where was that person who would love unconditionally, without any promises and expected standards? Would she have got it from the mother she had never known?

Goutu decided she would. She did not at that moment consider that she herself was so critical of her two daughters, that nothing they ever did satisfied her, leaving her longing for more, leaving them feeling empty, angry, confused. She decided that, had her mother's life been granted to her, Goutu, she would have been complete, whole, not in eternal search. The baby kicked again and Goutu got up from her chair. The house looked what it was, uninhabited, cold, without a centre. There were no young voices talking in hushed whispers, no one to answer her call, no one to rush to her rescue when she, in a fit of self pity, shouted with rage.

This baby would be with her till she died. She wasn't going to let anyone do anything to it, or come between her and the child. This was her insurance against age and loneliness. With this baby she would never be lonely again, nor would she be ever cut off from her moorings, that old house in which her grandfather lived, with its large hall, on which were portraits of the venerable members of her family, in full regalia, complete with turbans and black coats. She thought of the house now, she who had no home but held on fiercely to thoughts of this house which had banished her and Krishnanand and Achyutan to some distant fastnesses and those privileged to stay behind had been included in the glow of homehood. There were lovely spaces in that house, with its permanent kolams in the place where the gods and goddesses were hung, with their garlands of the malli Madurai boasted of. She could almost get in her nostrils, evocative and pungent, the smell of the sandalwood and incense that hung in the air.

I certainly got what I wanted, dears, there is no one now in my life except her, born as she was, gentle and feeble like the kicks she gave inside, she could do no more than just look at me when she was born and that is the way it remained. She lay there, not turning, not crawling, not sitting. Placid and unmoving she was, though I knew

I think even when she was inside of me that there was something different this time Though when we went to the doctor and he gave his verdict, I felt a cold wind pass over my heart, I saw the ice falling over all my life, staying white and hard for the rest of it. I can tell you now how I felt at that moment, when the doctor told us that she would not be like other children.

I remember the first time I saw ice falling, when soon after I got married I went up to the remote Himalayas, after travelling all the way from Delhi. I remember the snowflakes, pure and clean, falling like rain, but silently, making no noise, covering everything with white, covering even the branches with a white shine, as if a master painter had taken a giant brush and blanched the whole landscape with white. But the real cold came with the melting of the snow, then your very bones got chilled, till they were ready to wrench themselves off your body.

And so when I heard what the doctor had to say of this limp body with its wonderful face, yes my dears, there was always an expression of perfect understanding on her face and an inner light which could only emanate from this, I had the same feeling of chilled bones, as if some part was being torn off and there was to be no replacement for that part.

That night and many nights after this, the scenes that happened before her birth flashed across my mind in unending succession and she lying by my side, too weak even to turn, would suddenly make a noise, until one day she called me Amma just like that, but with great effort, she couldn't speak my dears like you and I can, she still can't and people think she can't understand what they are saying. But I can tell you that she even divines what they are thinking because she has this understanding that started from the womb. But let me tell you that carrying her to her birth was not easy and bringing her forth was a test, the girls had come to help me, my husband was raw with fear, fear had abraded his usual reserve and his mind, always so sharp, had clouded over with the dullness of tamas.

She had been cursed for speaking the truth while still in the womb, the truth being that none of us really understood the deeper existentials of life, I see that now, but then dears, I am now over eighty and the tapestry which we call life, the small details which give us grief or joy no longer signify.

I look over the rich colours my life has woven and realize that I could not have chosen these colours or these intricate patterns myself. There are dragons, rakshasas and rakshasis, the silk aunt, alive even when this child was born, Krishnanand's father who visited me when I went to Madras with her and even my father who looked at me wordlessly when I told him what the doctor had said. Their faces come before me even now, as I tell you this and I think back on these events, the dirty colours of Subra, with the embroidery in large uneven stitches, which even time cannot and will not wash out, the beautiful grandson and the grand daughters that life has lent me, my daughters and their husbands, and towering over all that, in the richest purple and gold, are my travels in search of liberty, for her and for me, when I crossed the seas and sailed away to find the answers to each of my questions.

But what can I say dears, that all of it has been a search, that every time I have had to go after the answers, why did Valli and Narayani and the others, Kamakshi for example, have all the answers served up to them in a silver tray?

I would give you an answer if I knew it.

Krishnanand

Sitting in a train to Calcuttta and looking out of the window at the mist filled semi darkness somewhere between Jabalpur and Calcutta, Krishnanand saw that his travels had covered a great distance. He had come a long way from his Sridevi days and had arrived at a destination unbeknown even to himself. This was one of the many stops he had been forced to make since his youth, ah! those heady days when his phallic powers had been in constant demand by his little cousins, those girls, now grandmothers, and not ready even to spare him a look. On his latest visit to Madras, he had visited Narayani and she had stood at the door, not opening it because she could not make out that it was her cousin, that god who had made love to her in what seemed like a century ago, just before her wedding, and she the next day being led as a lamb to slaughter. Narayani, who with the others would wait for his arrival as far outside the house as convention would allow, that day had screwed up her eyes against the sun and asked who he was!

'I'm Krishna, Nani,' he had said, using the old pet name which she loved to hear from him.

'Come in,' was her only reply. She was going backwards and forwards in that room, and would not rest till her grandson arrived from school. She rose when he wheeled his cycle in, and looked enquiringly at this stranger.

'My cousin, my mama's son,' Narayani had said. 'Your mama.' And she had looked at him. Krishnanand had noticed with distaste that her teeth were yellow. He tried hard to locate that slim girl of the pavadai and davani in this shapeless, grey haired woman. Lost in the whirlpool of time.

As if reading his thoughts, Narayani said, 'I didn't recognize you because you have put on so much weight. You used to be so tall and slim! We have all become old.'

Krishnanand looked down at his tummy. Yes, there was a belly, from drinking too much beer. He must give it up. He could not allow himself to run to seed. He was in Jabalpur with all its merrymaking and partying, there were plenty of women who didn't mind a flirtation or more with an unattached, childless divorcee.

Now Narayani was busy with the idlis, she had to serve her grandson his tiffin, would he like some? Curbing his first impulse to refuse, he said he would like some of her idlis served up with sambhar. The first mouthful confirmed that she had not lost that touch. The idlis were like malli poo, jasmines, soft, succulent and they melted in the mouth, the sambhar, redolent with freshly-ground spices, took him back as nothing else could have done to that old house by the river Vaigai, with its vast hall and pictures of venerable family members, turbans and all, his forbears, from whose loins he had sprung but to whose home he had no right, and whose house was the closest he had come to having a home. He suddenly recollected the kolams in the puja rooms and what was that scent coming into his nostrils with the sambhar podi? Yes it was incense and sandalwood and there was the old man, his grandfather, the repository of power and music, singing every morning of the grandeur of Meenakshi and Kamakshi and Visalakshi of distant Kashi. He could hear the rattle of the coffee filter in the kitchen, the parijarakam, the cook, always male, you could not have a woman with her monthly periods desecrating a house where goddesses were being worshipped.

When Narayani asked if he wanted one more, he said yes unthinkingly, if only to prolong the memory of the old home, that graciousness, with its lambent lights, there was no electricity for a long time, though now surely there would be, the beauty of it all.

And then he went up, with the eye of his mind, up those stairs to the only room reserved for honoured guests, leading on to a terrace where in the summer would dry all those delicacies called vadams, and at other times be used by him to laughingly dally with one of the little girls who came up on some pretext or other to admire his beauty.

Sitting here in this house, close to the temple of Karpakambal in Mylapore, he wondered why he had thrown it all away. What had his search been? For it was all a search, that much was clear

So when Goutu had confessed to him that there had been a hurricane in her life caused by a certain Subra, he had looked down, he had not wanted her to see the sudden spurt of anger he had felt. She had mistaken this for disapproval.

'Do you think I am bad?' she had asked and searched his face for an answer.

'I think you are human,' he had replied and had felt a great force of love for her. There had been no trace of lust in it, this was a new emotion.

Krishnanand wondered if this was what he had been looking for, this desire to protect rather than exploit.

He lay down on his berth. All this philosophizing gave a man a headache. He just hoped the Subra affair was over and done with.

Goutu

As I think I told you my dears, there was a secret that I had hit upon and that is that none of the others were fighting life, they were all submitting to it, and that is why their solutions appeared as if they were served up on silver trays. When like me you are on a search for answers, you have to get all the dross beaten out of you before the gold appears.

Though I still don't know if the gold has appeared.

Now that I sit here and contemplate Yama, he knows the way, dears, he has been to this house once already, my husband was taken away by him and so were Krishna and Achyut. Narayani and Valli have already gone and there is now only Kamakshi left. And of course I am sitting in this chair, getting dragged around .I am unable to decide what I feel about the final ending. And I have seen a lot of endings dears, but this needs thinking about.

I can tell you about them. There was the end of my pregnancy and the end of life as we knew it. Very cruelly the axe, the king of instruments, fell on our lives. We called her Meera, beloved of the divine cowherd. I haven't told you the names of the others dears, but that doesn't matter .You don't have to know people's names, life is a river which washes away as it creates. Anyone who comes in the way of its course, people like me or Achyut or Krishnanand. All the others run off with their things and get saved.

When I looked at her, I sometimes wondered at the difference between her face and its expression and the wasted body which had to be helped to do even the simplest things. At other times, I despaired at my desire to make her like everyone else, why should her legs hang limply, why should her tongue not utter the simplest sounds, why should she not be able to make her brain obey her body's commands?

The doctor had said that she would not do any of these things unless we taught her to do them. But how do you teach a bird to fly, a wave to move towards the shore, a child to walk?

My husband was on the rack, he felt his life was ruined, he could not do anything except blame us both for what he called the folly of having another child. The girls were speechless, they had long left the home and its concerns, they fell on me weeping with helplessness, they were afraid of what the future held. And all the time, I was responsible for her.

As I look at her now, I can't believe the twists and turns my life has taken. The search for the right answers—for her. I wanted her to be like everybody else to look at, to talk to. There must be no departures from the ordinary, no one must look or speak differently. Her legs must support her the way we understood legs to be, her thinking must be expressed in the way that we understood expression. Nothing must be out of line. Or you attracted looks and words of sympathy expressed in a way that made you cringe. I looked down at her sleeping face sometimes and wondered what was going through her head. A thousand thoughts were going through mine, was it possible that her head was entirely devoid of thought? What did her sudden, lovely smile hold behind it? When her hand gripped mine, what did she want to say?

You know dears, in later years, we went in a ship to England, to that white man's land far, far away and I saw and heard many things which made me understand myself better.

But the thing I want to tell you now is about what I learnt from their trees. Then when I came back with her, I saw it in our trees too. And this is it—in a forest of trees no two are alike. As I gazed up when I took her on walks and that is where I learnt to do this, I stopped going for walks when we came back, I thought that the beauty of the trees came from the differences, not the sameness. Now you tell me my dears, why do we think that if people do not look or behave or do the same things that others do in the same way and at the same time, they are lacking in something that others have to give them? Now you think about this, because I have thought and thought and not come to an answer.

Dharmakka did not understand what I was telling her about Krishna because it was different, my husband came to despair when he found that I was not one of his village girls though he had left his village behind, my mother-in-law did not understand her husband who liked freedom better than bondage, and now my daughter was being called names because she had not said the words or done the things she must do.

And as I said, we went in a large ship, yes, I crossed the seven seas just so that I could help her to walk and talk. What a dream that seems to be now! There was ice and snow everywhere, and I had to take her to the doctor and there was more than that.

There were new faces, new colours, new smells, new sights. And I on my own! The girls and my husband did not come with us.

As I sit here, more than thirty years after it all happened, after we took another ship and returned, I look down at my hands that did all the work which made our lives move across the seas. My hands are bent and twisted now, were these the hands that flew up and down on the strings of the violin? Yes and no. There was a tree in the woods where she and I went for walks, she on her chair with wheels and I walking behind her, pushing it and that tree looked as my hands looked now, large knobs, resembling the mane of a lion covered the trunk of the tree and the tree stood, roots in the earth, branches spreading, growing taller and taller, and we couldn't see the top of it. My hands now look like that treetrunk, but underneath lies the same fingers which seemed to have a life of their own.

There we both would sit, she looking on, and speaking to me about her school, yes she had been trained to speak, and I listening to her, with a pang in my heart for the other two who had tried to tell me about their school but I had not listened. When had that been and why does time play such tricks with us? Long ago and far away there had been two girls who had listened to my every word as their command and watched me with so much love and what had I done in return?

Nothing. It had all been an illusion. An illusion too, to think that life is as we want it, nothing waits dears, the river flows on, we had come a long way from its source, we were nearing its mouth and we must fall into the ocean before long. But wait! If the river falls into the sea, then it must return to land as rain.

So we have a chance with the gentle falling rain, which takes us back to the source of our lives, as I have seen with the drops falling as the Kaveri or the Godavari start in their mountain hide-outs, waited patiently for by men and women who close their eyes in silent prayer, while bells ring and camphor is waved, and then those lights are held in the faces of the worshippers, who gather it up with their respectful hands and touch their eyes and heads with it.

Seshadri

Seshadri came home with the tickets in his hand, they were to leave for England in a month's time. There was a doctor, located for his expertise in this surgery and he would do his very best to see that this child would walk. Seshadri had by now learnt the futility of planning ahead with a wife like Goutu and had surrendered his life into the hands of the gods.

Goutu took those tickets in her hands and looked at them.

Tilbury Docks, it said. Where was this place? Fear entered her heart, clouding the anticipation she had felt. She thought that night of the evening Krishnanand had come to bid their grandfather goodbye, he was going to England and she would have gone with him, at fifteen, if he had only said the word. But at forty five, she felt fear. What a journey it had been, these thirty years, what places she had seen, people she had met, but the inner core had remained unchanged.

Seshadri had given up the fight, he realized that there was to be no change from the imaginings, the make-believe and in the last two years, at over fifty, was beginning to feel the need to withdraw. It had been an illustrious career, spanning three decades, he would stay on for a few more years and then bid the whole thing goodbye. Never loquacious, he was becoming even more silent now. After the affair of Subra, he had given up praying in an organized way, but now many of the childhood prayers, for which he had been trained by his grandfather, were coming back to his lips. Chiefly, the gayatri. Only the other day he surprised himself by saying

Om bhur bhuva suvaha

And then going on to add

Ojosi sahosi balamasi brajosi

Thou art the essence of strength, thou art patience or the subduing power....

and so on.

He caught himself looking at the pictures in their puja room, yes that tradition had not waned, everything looked as if polished with gold, with the oil lamp throwing a dark but lambent shadow on the face of Venkateshwara, her chosen ideal. The silver container with the vibhuti was brought out every night and applied on the forehead of the child and on her tongue, where resides Saraswathi, the goddess of learning and the wife of Brahma.

He no longer thought that doing namaskarams to him would be equivalent to doing them to the god who found his home in the heart of his devotee. He now wanted to be left alone to wind up his affairs and move from the seat of power, a seat which had lost its significance and much of its meaning in the last five years, since the child had been born.

No he wasn't disgusted, he told himself, it was a natural desire, something like that of a leaf's, to turn from bright and glossy green to becoming yellow, waiting to be shaken off the tree, or of a river which loses its speed as it reaches the mouth and final destination, content to majestically flow, taking with it the waste of the banks, scarcely glancing at the people on either side, nor conscious of the weight of the boats which skimmed upon its surface. Yes he must start loosening his bonds, he decided and he would start by acknowledging that he had failed in his role as a husband.

Many were the ways in which a man might fail in his chosen path and all too often, Seshadri had gone over in his mind at the various things he had done or had not done, chief among these was whether he had chosen the right path on that distant day when her father had begged him to keep her, with both his hands held to his forehead. Seshadri had never forgotten that gesture, it had the power to bring home to him the full extent of his thrall over his father-in-law, merely by virtue of being his daughter's husband. He had come down even in his strictures over his visits, there was some money trickling in even now, but Seshadri had let go.

Narayanan

In a day or two Narayanan, now approaching eighty, grey and bent, holding off reconciliation with Achyutan who had accused him of sleeping with his wife, Narayanan's daughter-in-law, was due to arrive, to say his goodbyes to his daughter, embarking upon the long journey.

Narayanan did not approve: he thought his son-in-law was making a mistake. The two girls were still unmarried, the elder one nearly twenty-five and the younger one not too far behind, and the mother not in the house. Seshadri was not worried. True, he had given the matter some thought, one of his cousins had warned him of the dire consequences of girls who did not get married on time.

'Enna da, when are you getting them married?' he had asked.

Lightly for him, Seshadri had said 'Oh what is the hurry?',

The cousin had launched into a long story of various families in the village who had lost their daughters to men of a lower caste whom they had met in the course of their studies.

'Be warned, nothing good can come of this,' he had said.

Seshadri did not reply. His cousin would have been appalled at Seshadri's real reason for not getting his daughters married. It was his considered belief that daughters took after their mothers and he would not have been able to walk up to either son-in-law and hold his hands in supplication the way his father-in-law had.

He must loosen the knots of the heart and start preparing for his retirement and his move, not for him the cringing for other positions, he would go away, and would start by sending Goutu to England. Let whatever good come out of it or not, they must leave. He would decide what to do with himself, if not with them.

Goutu reached England one blustery winter day and in her sari and slippers she made an odd sight. Everything about the venture was like a landmine. She did not know anybody and she must get to a northern city where the doctor practised. Being the creature of unreason that she was, and her fears forgotten in the excitement of the voyage, the whole thing seemed to her like an adventure, the adventure of her life and she was going to do her best.

It was a fresh start and nothing seemed impossible, the surgery, the expense, the loneliness, the weather—all of it was tinged with the colour of red, of danger, of dare-devilry, of challenge, of passion.

This was what she had been waiting for all of her life, being left alone to do what she liked, without overseers, markers, expectations. She looked around her, the mini-skirts and the body revealing clothes, the open shows of affection in the streets and she realized that there was a state in which other people lived, where the only responsibility one had was to oneself, if that.

This discovery was the start of other painful growth-discoveries, in her mid-forties she learnt that while all the time she had been holding life responsible for herself, it was she and her actions, emanating from her knowledge of herself, which made growth possible

She gazed down the bridge, on her way home, at the river which flowed under it, bubbling with an inner life, as if from some inexhaustible inner, underground fount and felt she had never seen anything so beautiful. Many times, she would stand there and watch the ducks and the swans, winding their way down the river, in silent, slow grandeur, and marvel at the wonder of it all. She cast her mind to the rivers she had so far known, the Ganga, the Yamuna, the Godavari, the Kaveri, and she felt here there was something different, the waters seem to be coming from some stationary point just below the bridge, and in her rivers they came from some source far, far away. Grand, majestic, non-committal, uncaring. The river she saw below her now was of the moment, it did not seem to have a source or an ending, it flowed past right before her and seemed to symbolize her life in the country.

The sudden gusts of wind, the sudden sharp spells of rain too were the same. They were not menacing floods of water, large clouds, thundering and disgorging themselves for days, as an Indian monsoon rain might, they did not follow a procession of endlessly hot days, they were all of a piece, a gentle shower from low clouds scudding across the skies, falling on earth which was already drenched with dew, her ill-shod feet sinking into the receiving earth. She thought of her own country where rain fell on parched land, after the scorching summer sun had played mercilessly with the fields, cracking them with dryness, so that when the clouds finally opened, it was as if the thirsty earth could not have enough of their waters.

Her unalloyed Indian-ness, her views expressed directly and without care for form or tact found her friends who wondered at the incongruity between her appearance and her stout courage and many times, the sight of Goutu pushing a chair with wheels, almost running away with her, drew more than a glance.

It was a nurse at the hospital who first gave her an idea of her own achievement.

'You are right brave, you are!' she said one morning.

'Who me?' asked Goutu. She was incredulous, no one had thought her brave. She was always being told how difficult she was.

'Yes,' said the nurse. 'We don't reckon that any of us would go so far from home with a child as you have done, luv.'

Yes you would, thought Goutu, if like me you had found that as a result of your actions everyone you knew had had their lives turned over, you would go far away to make amends.

All right dears, so I suppose the question is: then why did I return to this life, if I found that one where I was at last my own mistress.

I can tell you the answer to that.

There is, in the heart of every person, a central part which is given away as one goes through life's journey and this heart has to be divided into many pieces to sustain this charitable dispensation of its constituent parts. And so it is that we go through our lives with our many loves and hates, those raga-dweshams, which colour our responses and make us act in this way or that, reply to one, ignore another, like my aunt of the silks and shaking diamond earrings, who turned her back on me when she served her own daughters with maternal attention

Or like Chitti who served my father with watered down buttermilk and treated Achyut with such laughingly served up contempt that a boy could not even understand what it meant, while her own vibhuti-washed sons got the love in her eyes.

Giving away pieces of this heart, physical in nature, is as vital as the heart itself, and is as innate to human nature as the heart itself is. It was part of my aunt's heart that I had craved, but she would give me no piece of it. It was Achyut's desire and Krishnanand's too that they might be worthy of this gift, the only but the most valuable gift, on this journey. None of us got this and so it was that we did not know to give our own love away. The desires, the hankerings, the lies, the scattering as of spilt mustard seeds, which cannot be gathered up again, had their beginnings in this withheld heart.

In this country of adoption, which had been my home for some years, with just the child and I looking at each other across the table, my pushing the chair with the wheels, sitting under trees, listening to her speak, watching her even learn to walk, without having to pretend to be happy or unhappy, without the opposites of good-bad, true-untrue, right-wrong, living my own life, on my own terms, in my own way, without the pretence of acting a part, many things came together to bring this physical heart, located in the rib-cage, and beating of its own volition, with no prompting from anybody, not even its owner, to an understanding of why it was there at all.

It wasn't there to beat this way and that, or to flit from flower to flower like a great red and black butterfly, or to hop from branch to branch like an ignorant bird. It was there to sustain the owner, give her life and strength.

And so, I returned home, a home which had been fractured and had dissipated, which had moved from the dusty northern climes, which had seen me arrive as a girl, dissatisfied and untried, made me a woman who, in her search for herself, had lied and kicked and fought her way to understanding and learning.

When Goutu returned with Meera, she had expected an effusive welcome from the girls, though she knew Seshadri well enough to realize that he would do no more than just say 'So you are back!' to the child. She did not get the welcome she had imagined, the two girls had gone their own ways with no help or aid from her and they had now anesthetised the part which had yearned for her presence, that exciting, unpredictable, demanding, tantalizing presence, which had wielded so much influence over their growing years.

Their period of banishment from their home had coincided almost exactly with their forays into the outside world which they had found themselves dismayingly ill-equipped to understand.

There had been many changes, the cousin's predictions had come true and the girls were now married to men of their own choosing with children of their own. Goutu found her home broken in more ways than one, Seshadri unable to hold the home and its contents together, had given away everything that Goutu had so painstakingly put together.

'Where are the cups and saucers with the rose pattern?' she had asked.

Seshadri did not reply. He had had no use for cups and saucers when he was in distant Delhi and he had even less use for them now.

'Did you hear me?' she asked.

The chair with the wheels, lovingly brought back from across the seas, stopped in its tracks. The child did not know, had forgotten, it seemed to Seshadri, what living in a home was like.

He flung the paper down. She was making him angry.

What? Had she still got the power to do that?

Yes she had. She would not lose her spell over all of them. Only last week one of the girls had come home and there had been furious whisperings. The girl had left for her own home with a sullen and mutinous expression. Seshadri understood it to be a battle of wills.

'If you wanted all the cups and saucers intact, you should have been there to pack for the move!' he shouted, his eyes glinting behind their glasses.

Goutu went back. Yes the move. The move had been to Madras, Seshadri had left the north without even looking back, he blamed his exile for many of the games life had played on him and he had firmly turned his back on that unfriendly place, with its many enticements.

Goutu had not minded. What was it about after all? All these comings and goings and all the pressures, the vile rivalries, the chairs and tables and carpets and curtains.

Suddenly her mind did a flip and went back twenty years.

Maya! What had become of her? And Khudiram? Khudida—that's what she used to call him. What an odd day it had been when they found out that he was the son of a seamstress who had escaped Chittagong's massacres. Goutu looked out of her kitchen window. How important it had all seemed! That chair that Maya owned was the one thing she had most wanted at the time.

In her new-found understanding, which she had to admit deserted her when she most needed it, she thought she would let go of the cups with the roses. She would go to the bank where Narayanan had left some money for her and buy some cups.

Narayanan! Even he had at last left her, a lonely broken man, who had tried his best to remain true to his wife and had lost his children in the process. She recalled the day she had received the news, it had been by cable, specially delivered. She went into her chest of memories and took this one out. She had been summoned by the chief of the hospital where she was working to be near the child.

She had entered her room with a beating heart. She found the English, her country's overlords for so long, intimidating. And, truth to tell, she didn't quite follow what they said. The lady rose from the chair and came over to where she was standing. Goutu was even more confused. What was this? Were they to be told to go home?

'Sit down,' the lady said. 'Can I get you some tea?'

'No,' said Goutu, and added as an afterthought, because she was still not used to their niceties, 'thanks.'

Her fear rose to choke her.

Then a moment later, she heard the lady speak.

'I have some bad news for you,' she said. 'Your father has died, luv.'

'My father?' Goutu had repeated.

The lady looked at her. 'It is a shock, in't?' she said.

A shock? Goutu couldn't answer. It was the end of another chapter in her life, this lonely man's widowed existence, her grandmother's entry into their lives when they had all been left bereft of support, his empty house, his unsmiling face except for the keen looks and the half-smiles he allowed himself, the silences, his defeat.

'How did you know—that he is dead?' she asked.

The lady handed her the cable.

It was brief but she had sat down and gone over the years, those years which had held nothing for her except solitariness, she had no memories of any kind which she could laugh about, and then her mind turned to her wedding day. What a lot of tears she had shed, everyone thought it was because she was leaving Pati and Narayanan. Then she thought of the bureau, funnily enough Seshadri had saved it and it was right there in her latest home, with some bumps and dents to show for its much-travelled state. She remembered the camphor lights and the payasam and her heart felt like lead.

But the sharpest memory was Narayanan holding Seshadri's hands to his head. When that image came to her mind, she wept for the orphan she had become.

Later, one of her daughters who was in Madras, wrote that Achyutan Mama had been found, drunk but compliant, to do the rites. So Achyut could add this to his list of those he had dispatched. But this time, it was no river down which he had sent the urn. It was the vast, monstrous sea, the sea which laces Madras on its eastern side, with its treacherous waves and sudden dips, which swallowed the mortal remains of Narayanan. He was gone, with no trace, with no ado. Much like his own self.

Thirteen days later, Achyutan had gone back to wherever he lived, she did not know, but somewhere in Madras, which can house any old wreck. Goutu was at her post, having pushed down all her old life somewhere in the darkest part of her being, that old life which had so much power to hurt, but was powerless, through the action of the wheel of time which turns without help from anybody, to come back.

Krishnanand was packing up, he was leaving Bhopal where he had been living these ten years or more and wending his way home. Krishnanand had no roots anywhere but he had a house not far from Narayani's and through one of the twists of fate, had decided that that this would be home now.

The move had been forced upon him. He pushed down the memory of the humiliating meeting with his immediate boss and told everyone that 'A man has to know when to call it a day.' Polite smiles had greeted this airy remark of his and he knew that everyone knew the real reason.

He consoled himself with the thought that in Madras it would be de rigueur—a man must use these little French expressions—to wear chappals and—veshti? No. He had not worn one for ages. Perhaps not since he attended the marriages of all those cousins of his. After his days in England, he had thought of it as a dress of the farmer, and Gandhiji had really brought the veshti into disrepute with his half-naked appearance. He would not wear the veshti.

He looked around this large house, one he had been given by the government.

It was completely empty now, save for the waste of the life of a decade spent here. He didn't have very much, the usual utensils, the regulation furniture, which he was leaving behind, he had very little to call his own, the clothes and some books, some other odds and ends, his belongings mirrored his life—disconnected, frayed, impersonal.

He sat down in one of the chairs which were in the huge drawing room as it was called and realized that it was like every other chair he had ever sat on. There had been no changes or differences in his life, no markers, such as the birth of children or their achievements, or the death of someone close, his father was still living and the others didn't signify. There! Again that empty, sinking feeling. The sheer pointlessness of it all, the aridity, the waste came to him like a slow and lazy wave trying to make it to the shore.

Never one to enjoy looking into himself, he jumped from the chair and in doing so, caught sight of himself in the mirror just above the opposite chair. He hurriedly looked away, he knew the fell, defacing hand of time, aided by his own excesses, had more than wrought changes in his face and body. That curly hair had thinned, the body, in contrast, had thickened, his face had loose flesh hanging from the sides, giving him the appearance of an old fox. Gross, unattractive, and he, who had relied on his physical attractions as the mainstay of his life, realized that he was being left unarmed, as if the gods had systematically conspired to weaken him in order that he might be defeated, and he was being defeated. The last few times, his conquests had been much dyed, parchment-skinned women, their make-up not quite hiding those lines of dissatisfaction, their droopy breasts, most off-putting, some of them as cigarette-staled as he himself was. The younger women did not even look his way, there were other younger men who had stepped into his position both in the game of seduction as well as into his professional shoes. His bosses were younger and men who no longer took a lenient view of his sexual escapades. One of them had actually summoned him.

'How would you like to move, Mr Krishnanand?' he had asked.

Move? No. He felt a new lethargy which did not allow him to go to a new place and begin afresh. He did not want to move, it was too tiring.

'Well, actually…' he began.

'I think,' said the young man, 'you may have to. We have had some complaints.'

What? This was new. He felt a righteous rage at this youngster's words. He would have exploded but he had to keep silent.

'How do you mean?' he asked.

'Mr Krishnanand, I have instructions to tell you that it may be better if you choose to get transferred. That way you will be able to stay on in the department.'

Was the man telling him that he would be sacked? Then it was better he thought about leaving and licking his wounds in private.

But where would he go? Not Delhi, it had become an ocean of babudom and red-tape, no-one knew anybody and the new breed were not sophisticated enough for a half-Englishman.

Then?

Madras?

He would have to think about it.

Sitting in this chair, and on the wrong side of the table, with no respite in sight, trying to feint with his own thoughts, this way and that, he heard some words echoing his own.

'...think about it,' the voice was saying. 'There is no hurry. The decision can be made in a month.'

So a deadline was being given him. The young man had just nodded his head and Krishnanand felt the finality of his dismissal.

He got up, turned and left.

Back in his cavernous quarters that evening, Krishnanand sat at his usual spot. One of the boys brought out his drink and placed it on the table next to him.

He was lost in thought—what had it all meant anyway?

Nothing. All of it was lost in the well of time. No use going down that road, that was so futile.

He would go to Madras. He had a house there. Perhaps there, with the cool evening breezes of the sea, the language of his mother and his mother's mother in his ears and on his tongue, orgasmic joy might once more be his.

He looked down at his now empty glass.

None of this was true and he knew it. In the packing he had come upon some old photographs and had been choked with nostalgia when he saw his old images, images weaving in and out with the past, just as dappled sunlight plays with water, now a shadow, now a brightness. The young man of the heavy-lidded eyes, the desirable body, of the infinitesimal pleasures had gone and nothing could replace it.

He flung his glass down and it fell, tinkling into a thousand rainbow coloured pieces, the fumes of the rum that was left in it rose in the air and he got up from the chair. One of the boys was there to help him, another wiped up the mess.

'I can't put the glass together again,' he mumbled incoherently and realized even in his alcohol-induced craze that he was talking about his life.

Achyutan

Achyutan looked around this room, his home for the last four months. In the many years he had lived in Madras, rooms like this had been home. He had moved in with his father, but no, that had been a lunatic period in his life, he had wanted several explanations from his father, none of which had been forthcoming.

Why had his father made him kill that beautiful lady of the long fingers and blue-veined skin whose complexion had a sparkle which vied with the diamonds in her ears? Why had it been his duty to set fire to her and then, at his father's and grandfather's orders, pick up a mud pot which he had then submerged into the Vaigai?

What about the banishment to the cow-shed of his Chitti? He recalled the whining and the half-smiles of his father's voice and her laughing, dodgy answers. And then why had he made him marry those smoky grey eyes, with the same blue-veined breasts, whom he could only bed, but not get nearer to than that?

And what about Dharma and her end? Why was he made to play a part in everybody's end? He could not remember even one occasion when he had started at the beginning, he was always part of the middle, he must join whatever was happening without having his say.

He put his glass down. He was being forced to drink filthy stuff, liquids that were burning his throat as they went down, but drink them he must if he were to go down the labyrinthine ways of his mind. He looked down one serpentine path, tried to take a few tottering steps and gave up, it was too dark, he could not see and discrimination, that which is the light of the inner eye, had been blown out by the many storms raging in his heart.

He opened another door, creaking with age and disuse, and there seemed to be an illumination somewhere, dare he go and see what awaited him there? Yes, he must. He must make peace with himself. The young girl who was leaving the house in her bridal finery was Goutu. Why was she looking so unhappy? Krishna was leaving, walking down the stairs, his smile intact despite his banishment.

He had said something, yes, he remembered it now, he had told him, that he could not come to the wedding, Goutu would not be allowed to see him. He did not want any scenes here, the bridegroom's party were already here and they were not to know anything.

Did I do the right thing then, Achyutan wondered. Did I have the right to play with Goutu's life? I dismissed her whole life by sending away Krishna and ordering her to go in. On such momentary actions do whole lives hinge. So Goutu spent her whole life away from the one person who meant anything to her, and why did Krishna also find himself like a wanderer, a sliver of his life here and another there.

And I?

That did not bear consideration. Not a single relationship had fructified, or assumed the golden sheen of a well-worn silk garment. All of them had a rent here, a tear there, some were torn right down the middle, irreparable, to be discarded.

How now to mend them? How put the stitches in place?

Achyut looked out of the window to the shabby roofs opposite, there was not even a tree to relieve the monotony of the windowscape. Was it for this that he had been brought to this world, to leave without even a trace?

He did not know anything about his children, he had surmised that they were in the same city as he, but where were they really? Were they married? Was he, even as he swirled this sharp liquid which burnt his tongue and throat with its acrid acidity, a grandfather?

Grandfather. Nice thought, I must say, Achyutan spoke to himself in his own mind as he had always done, but with the colours of his earlier expression now dimmed, I wasn't even a proper father. What was it about time that it went through ones fingers like salt, turning black hair to white, smooth skin to wrinkles, changed seasons and made little leaves fall off trees, silently fluttering through the air as he himself now was doing, waiting to fall to the ground? Would the landing be painless? He hoped so.

Had the old man gone with a thud? He remembered the knock on the cheap wooden door of his earlier lodgings, was it two before this one, or three? Can't remember, thought Achyutan. Well anyway that does not matter. Someone had come in and it was about midnight. He had heard shouts and loud knocks, they had been knocking a long time and the lodge owner was furious, the other guests would wake up.

From somewhere deep down, from that subterranean world of desperation and forgetfulness, consciousness had surfaced. He had got to the door, opened it and looked at the two men stupidly. The lodge owner had not been very subtle.

'Someone has died, they want you.'

Who?

The other man held out a note. It was from one of his cousins, so the bastards knew how to get him when there was dirty work to be done. They always pleaded ignorance when he had wondered why he wasn't ever contacted.

It was the old man. He had gone.

Achyutan looked at the note written in Tamil. It was rich with irony. He was born for the sole purpose of sending everybody down the river, it was a ritual started when he was four and here he was at nearly sixty, still at it.

He laughed, his laughter was almost a snigger, he had always been an embarrassed laugher, his inability to speak had been matched by his ignorance of the laughing process, the little tickle that reaches the brain, shakes a man to his feet and makes him shout with an understanding of the ludicrous. His writing was peppered by a wry sense of the funny, but that was part of his secret world.

The messenger was surprised. Achyutan was about to say, 'What has this got to do with me?'

He suddenly remembered his school where reading the Ramayanam was an everyday affair. When Hanuman had come to the court of the Raksasha king Ravana who had abducted Sita, the wife of the earthly Rama, who was in reality Vishnu, the Indweller of all, Ravana had wanted to kill him. Better sense had prevailed. His brother had reminded him that to kill a messenger was an act of cowardice and unbecoming of a monarch.

Why had that memory surfaced now of all times, at this moment? Was he going mad? He did not say the words that came to his lips.

He went in and came out again, having worn his shirt, ready to accompany this stranger, to accomplish what he had been born to do. He would give his father a send-off, in the pyre of his father he would see an apparition, haunting in her beauty, one of the blue-veined arms and long fingers, black hair done up in a single plait snaking down her back, with its little bunch of malli, ears sparkling.

He had gone to his father's house and once more the chilling loneliness of his father's life hit him. Some more cousins were there, the swines, and among them were Narayani and Valli.

Goutu was across the seas, they had not written or spoken or met for many, many years now, it was one of the legacies of homelessness, and Achuytan felt once more that hot liquid rushing up his throat, up, up, right through his skull, where it all congealed into a mass and settled on his brain, the parts which control speech, memory, love, the ability to feel pain. He looked round the room, only Valli retained the ability to look him straight in the eye.

Someone had given a veshti, he had sat on the floor, next to the man who had in a moment of lust given him life, the man who was now nothing but a body, a kattai, a piece of wood, he had put that man's head on his lap and whispered some meaningless words into his ears. He had then, accompanied by some of the cousins and one or two others, gone to the burning ghat, lit the pyre.

Then, still a prisoner of the priest and custom, he had stood with his back to the now burning body and with two bunches of darba grass held in his two hands, thrown them over his shoulders.

The next day, he had come back, collected some bones and the ashes, the mortal remains of the man who, with the overwhelming ignorance of the consequences of his own actions, had planted in his mother the seed of a man called Achyutan, the man he called appa, father, now put into a mud urn and, this time, he went to the sea which lies to the east of Madras and there, waist-deep in the impartial waters, had thrown the urn, to be carried away to the furthermost shores of infinity.

He could now walk away, it was all over. His last duties as a son were now accomplished.

Goutu

So there we all were, Krishnanand, my brother and I in the same city by the sea, all our lives having taken different paths, meeting now and again, like loops in a river, now running like three parallel roads in the city, each of us not really knowing what the other was doing. For a long time I didn't know Krishna was in Madras, he had not come to visit us and I had gone far, far away, so far away that I had left everyone behind.

One morning there was knock at the door and there was a young boy with a letter in his hand.

'Yaar, appa?' I asked.

'Goutami amma?' he said.

A letter again! No, I didn't want to open it. Letters had a way of taking life, they could bite, they were like swords, they could change life as we knew it. But the boy was waiting. I took the paper from him.

Who was it from? I thought I knew the writing, hadn't I seen it before?

My heart was thumping in my breast dears, this is something I can tell you happens to me even now, and I, over eighty! The telephone has only got to ring and my heart still beats faster as it does when the girls speak in a loud voice to show that they are angry with me.

It was from Achyutan!

'Dear Goutu', it said, 'I am not well. I want to see you once and talk to you. I know this might cause problems with SKS but if you tell this boy when I can come, I will be at your house at the right time.'

Achyutanna

I read that letter again, you know dears, it is very difficult to take yourself back to the position of a thangai, the younger sister, and by reading the word anna, I naturally became the sister.

Such is the power of words. They can take you back fifty, sixty years, they can bring back, sharp as a knife, the memories you thought your brain had forgotten. That knife can cut and draw blood too, it can tear your heart open, and blood can come out, till you beg it to stop. Even then, sometimes, that wound stays open.

I saw now that distant day when Krishna had come to take me away and Achyut had stood at the top of the stairs, at the door, and told him something that had made Krishna look in and then turn away and walk down the stairs.

Whatever it was he had said, my life's course had changed, inalterably.

But had it really?

How did I know even now if Krishna would have had the courage to say, All right Goutu, come away with me?

How could I think now that the girls and through them their lovely children, my grandchildren, beautiful they are, could be prevented from coming to this world through the actions of mere mortals? Were they all there, somewhere, waiting to be born, through the wheels of time, which has decided all our lives and the course that life must take?

Is this what Hari, the lord of the universe, the supreme leader who takes into himself everything, said in the battlefield to the confused Partha? That all of it is done, and that we ourselves are only agents? However it is, we think if only I had said that or done this, if only he had not done or said this or that, my life would have been that of someone else's.

As I looked down at this paper, torn from some old notebook, written in a writing which was difficult to read, I cannot tell you now what I felt. It is not important, but I remember what I did. I went with that boy to see him, sitting in a cycle rickshaw, the boy on a cycle just before me. Through some crowded lanes, just like Achyutan's life had been, now stood a lodging house, with men's clothes hanging from the walls, paint on the doors peeling off, as gross as Achyut's life had become was the place he now lived in. I sat in the rickshaw, unable to take it all into my sight, so I can't tell you everything now, how it looked because my eyes would not believe that one who I knew, had common blood with, was in this place. And as I looked at the posters, the roughness, someone called my name.

My brother! Are you that boy, who could not say much, who made pati weep, who spoke to our father words of such anger, who guessed what Krishna was going to do and sent him away, who officiated at my wedding, who sat with my children on his lap for their naming ceremony ? Then why are you looking so weary, what has life done to you? What choices did you make, that your eyes should be so full of grief?

I remember that smile, that same half-smile of our father, that grey hair, but surely it wasn't so grey when we met, most of all I remember that apology for living, walking on this earth, hiding behind a wall of self-deprecation, and I suddenly hear your voice.

No, it hasn't changed. That remains the same and I am taken back many, many years, to that Chitti's house, to Dharmakka's death, and to that old house by the Vaigai, where we all made believe that we had a family, just like everybody else. But only we didn't.

'You shouldn't have come here, I would have come to see you. This is not a place for you.'

He had wanted to tell me something. What was it? Had my father left a message for me?

'What did you want to tell me?' I asked.

I saw his eyes shining behind his glasses. His face, now changed by time, yet unchanged in its expression, looked at me.

'It's about what happened just before your wedding. I told Krishnanand to leave. I told him he could not meet you, that your wedding had been fixed and there could be no change How much did it change your life?'

'What did he say?' I asked.

'Nothing. But Dharmakka had told me, Goutu, I had promised her I would do something.'

Dharmakka!

I went back in the long ribbons of the road that I had taken, a step here, a few steps there, my husband walking steadfastly down the same road, the girls following, I walking down some other paths, then finding that I must go back to the self-same road that they trod on, looking, looking, searching in the hearts and lives of others what I could not find in my own, because I did not know it existed there, yes dears, it surely finds a place in your own hearts and minds, if you know that spiritual heart which lives six inches below your throat, yes, like this, just here.

Somewhere, far away, hidden by a curtain through which all of us pass every second of the day, I saw a young girl who had been undone by her own body and its betrayals, a vivid shining face, who lay there, getting thinner and thinner, who knew of the secrets of many things but who passed through to some other world before she could share them with us.

So she had told him. There had been someone who had cared about what might become of me.

Thinking about this now as I sit in this chair, with the winter landscape of that white man's land, faraway and long ago coming to me in my mind, I see suddenly a warm sun, shining at me with the colours of our own Indian summer, bright, orange and ochre, green and pale brown and against that white silvery sheen and I feel, what is it about my life that made so many colours come and go: green and purple and grey and red, in every shade and of every hue, that bright yellow which is called manjal, the blue green mazhil kazhithu, adorning a peacock's throat, smooth and velvety, and alongside that, running very close, the white of the country, so far away, across the seas.

He was looking at me at that moment, almost as if he held a silver plate in his hand to collect my words as they fell from my lips.

I couldn't answer. At that moment, my grief at losing Dharmakka, which I didn't feel when she actually went away, brought the tears to my eyes, caused them to fall, unchecked, heaving out of my body, as a cataract might fall from great heights.

'I'm sorry Goutu,' he was saying. 'I didn't know it had caused you so much unhappiness.'

So he thought I was weeping about Krishnanand.

Seri, let him. Let him think it. Whatever anyone thinks now, it is all over. I am Goutami, Goutami Seshadri. That is what I will remain till the end.

I can't remember what I answered dears, but that visit helped me to make up my mind.

My life had moved away from this man's, the boy I had known, while residing in this man of the crumpled shirt and thin grey hair, had lost his identity, thirty years lay between that boy and this person, and I? I, too, had changed. That girl who had been led to compress herself into a small space, as it were, who had been presented with sets of opposites, as if they were the only paths to understanding, was now this woman who had liberated herself with her actions, with her lies, which had the same power as other people's truths since they defined her, with her casting away in her mind of ways of thinking that were like life jackets to those floating in the waters of life. Not for this woman those pre-ordained, straight lines, those empty definitions of self. From the fractured past of non-relations, this woman had come out into another world.

My thoughts came suddenly back to the present. This voice was saying something.

'I did what I thought was right,'

I looked at him. You know dears, sometimes, I wonder what happens to all those old things which you think you are going to say at any given moment. They need not be said. Krishna and I had many things in common. We were united in our need for each other because of those things which we had left behind, which were denied us because of the aridity of others.

Now with the child, I thought, I had no further use even for Krishna. He could go, or he could be there. I had loosened the bonds of the heart. That is the way it was.

'It is all over,' I answered in Tamil. 'What use is this now?'

'You have become very wise,' he said. 'Is this from your husband?'

I did not answer. I said that I had to go. No further use for this man, either.

The mystery had been solved, the mystery of what might have been. There is no such thing. Things are the way they must be.

And so it was that when his messenger came a few months later and told me that he had been admitted into hospital, I could go with my heart in its place of rest, with my senses intact, to say goodbye to this brother of mine, this boy who had been treated as badly by life as he had treated her, as he lay dying, as his touch, smell, sight, taste and hearing left him, one by one and that light in the spiritual heart left by one of the orifices to join the great light that shines from the top of mount Meru.

My husband was with me, as the door of the van shut with a loud clang as the body made its way to the pyre. To this day, and I am over eighty now, I have no idea of who sent him to join the father he had despised and the grandfather he had feared, or the mother he idolized.

Achyutan's story had come to a close. When we turned to go, my husband leading and I behind him, not the usual thing dears, not at all, this time it was I who put the mortal remains of Achyut into the sea which is part of every human being's imagination, the sea of non-remembrance.

It was the loud ringing of the phone's persistence that woke Krishnanand .

It was Narayani.

'Achyut has gone,' she said

Wait a minute! Who is Achyut?

'Irrukiya?' said the voice on the other end. 'I know you two were close friends, but…!'

'Achyut?' As he said it, Krishnanand felt a huge jolt go through his body. Both the name and the import of the words entered his consciousness and made their way to his buddhi.

'When ?' he asked.

'Yesterday, Kamakshi phoned. It seems he died in the hospital and they took away his body directly from there. Just imagine! I don't know how they will do a thing like this. Don't know what Goutu was doing. Thank god that Periappa is not there to see all this! He would have...'

Krishnanand cut her off in the middle of more sentences which were ending with the exclamation marks of her shock and her inability to step outside the charmed circle of right-wrong, good-bad. His mind was also doing some funny gymnastics. He too would be put into just such a van and taken off, to be taken to the cremation ground without any preamble. Horrible thought.

Narayani was still speaking into his reluctant ear.

'...so though today is Tuesday, on the first ten days anyone can go because it does not matter, though if there is a widow, the tenth day is not allowed because that is the day she has to take off her...' her voice fell and stopped its excited chatter.

Thaali, he mentally supplied the missing word. That golden rope, the symbol of womanhood's ultimate achievement, proclaiming to the world that the humiliation of bride-viewing had had a successful end, that golden chain which binds in fetters both the wearer and the person who ties it. Krishnanand remembered for a tenth of a second the ludicrous scene of his own hands tying the thaali round Sridevi's neck.

And why was Narayani sounding so elated, was she reliving the day when her own colourless husband died, was one part of her thrilled to be the centre of all action at last, freed from the duties of catering to his every whim and that of his mother's, his vast family, demented by having to remain in a shadowed, cloistered world, not saying anything, not doing anything which would show the world who the real Narayani was?

'...so I am going now, before my bath because anyway we will have to do snanam as soon as we return, having gone to enquire about her grief. I have to come back and keep the cooker for my grandson, he has school. So will you come to my house in the next ten minutes?' At last, Narayani drew breath.

Krishnanand sat up in his bed.

'You go,' was all that he said.

'Then you?' she asked. 'Will you go on Sunday? That would be right. Go on a Sunday. It is the right day.'

'All right,' he said. 'I'll go on Sunday.'

Krishnanand put the phone down. He got up and made his way to the bathroom.

Coming back to the kitchen where, every morning, he made his lonely first tumbler of coffee, Krishnanand saw his life as one might watch a play unfold before one's eyes. He saw all those meetings as boys, in that large house by the river Vaigai, where his grandfather presided over affairs as the reigning deity of Madurai, Sunderaswarar, might reign over the heart of the queen of Madurai, the goddess Meenakshi. He was omnipotent, omniscient, omnipresent, Krishna had never felt so safe anywhere else as in the tutelage of his grandfather.

He had not thought of it as overweening arrogance that he had wanted to know everything that happened, indeed divined the truth.

Why had he, Krishna, not grown up in that house?

How might his life, and that of Achyut's, been different if they had had part of the shade of the grandfather's umbrella? What might have happened if his father had not gone in search of a western lifestyle to Madras, and there remarried?

And then those meetings with Achyut in Delhi. He had been aware that Achyut had tried, several times, to tell him about Goutu. He had resisted. What was it about his own power over women that had given him such a sense of being an overlord? And why had he revelled in that overlordship time and time again with all those girls, one by one?

And then the landlady's daughter in England He had left almost overnight when her mother told him that she was going to have a baby, his baby, He had thought it a lie, but he was too scared to stay.

Then Sridevi.

He had been unmanned by her. Emasculated. She had been the lesson he needed to learn.

But he hadn't really learnt it.

On and on it had gone, till it had the power to nauseate him. He recalled the way the young pisser had spoken to him that last month. Sickened he had been.

Narayani had now disturbed his daily routine with her allusions. Fleetingly he wondered then why they were not included in the family's observations of ritual. Did they think that he didn't care? He wanted to beg them to understand that he did. All his life he had longed to be part of that charmed, noisy circle, but he had been on the fringes, with Achyut and Goutu.

What made them different? He couldn't answer this question, he was thinking now of his own father's departure, last year.

He had been summoned in much the same way as had Achyut, to do his duties as a son. He had looked down at the old man, now placed on the floor, that sharp tongue now silenced forever, those frowns of disgust and intolerance replaced by the pall of death, of coldness and inactivity. His step mother and the children, now all grown up had been there and silently watched him. He had not spoken a word to any of them. They were not anywhere in his sight or earshot, he did not acknowledge their presence as cohabitors of the same planet.

He did nothing more than what by tradition had been required of him, merely officiating as the agent of departure, the person lending respectability to an event that had already taken place. For whether he would or not, his father had gone, carrying with him all his actions, his raga-dweshams, his prarabdhams, his sillinesses, his nobilities, his entire person in fact, all, all of it, except his body, which he, Krishnanand, his eldest son, consigned to the flames and having done this noble act, walked away without looking backward.

And now, Narayani.

My good cousin, he longed to shout, people like Achyutan or Goutu and even I have no prescriptions because we had to make our own rules or not make them. All those expectations can only be honoured by those who were in the framework. Our mothers left us to our own selves, they were not there to give us a part of their selves. In a mother lies the self, in a father only the seed, of the persons we become.

Hang it all, he would visit Goutu today, this afternoon, when he was in a better frame of mind, in Achyut's death lay the knell of his own. He felt a sudden drop in his spirits.

He would go now. He would find out the address from Narayani and go, she would have come back.

He dialled her number and she picked up the phone.

'Give me Goutu's address,' was all he said.

She gave it to him and he set off. He had not seen Goutu since her return from England. He could not recall any home thoughts, he had left it all so far behind him. He would catch up, Goutu, always effervescent, would tell him what he wanted to know.

Goutu

She was in the kitchen. Goutu found herself in a rage, brought on by the grief-enquiring visits of her cousins Narayani and, later, Uma.

As always, curiosity, not affection, was the basis of their visits. She was a curiosity. Whatever happened to her, to her life, and they were two different things now whereas before they were one and the same, her cousins had wanted to know as an aberration, as a departure from what they themselves, instructed as they were in the rights and wrongs of the thinking and acting process, would have done.

She knew now that there was, in the minds of those so instructed, a certain machine, ticking away like a clock, which rang like the same clock, preset for moments of uncertainty, so that by its ringing, they would be alerted to the consequences of their actions.

Only, in her life, this clock had been silenced forever by the death of a young woman in childbirth. That woman, the smell of whose death Goutu still held in her nostrils from that faraway day, lost for ever in the drainpipes of eternity, but the stench of that room with its amniotic fluid and blood was imprinted in the memory of every cell in her body. Stemming from that day, through her life, she had said and done things which had resulted in embarrassed silences, ugly scenes, near-death separations, lies.

Achyutan had died, that blood which had held them together, had frozen in his veins, the roundabout stopped, the red fluid that wove strange patterns in the body, now flowing faster, now slower, now turning cold, now warm and loving, bathing every part of one's body, the nourisher of the body and the mind and all the constituent parts which go to make up the whole.

The doorbell rang again.

With her in the kitchen stood Muniamma, her help, her confidante and the absorber of all her many comments about Seshadri and her worries about Meera.

'Paar,' she said. 'See who it is.'

Muniamma went off, muttering. She had found the whole thing shocking and had asked if Achyut had been her real brother. Goutu had looked angry and said 'Yes.'

'Then are you not doing the mourning in the correct way? Where are his wife and children?'

'Not with him. Forget this mourning, Muniamma.'

'Does he have a son?'

'Muniamma, what is this son, son, son? Yes he has a son. But what is the use?'

'Terrible. You are doing something wrong. It is very bad for your children and their children, especially that grandson of yours.'

'Muniamma, in sheemai, do you think every vellaikaran has his son standing by his side when he dies? No, he doesn't. Don't they somehow do something?'

'That's because they bury their dead. Here we are talking about agni. A son has to be present when his father is made one with agni. Otherwise, he will not leave this world, he will be like a ghost with unfinished business in this life, a kateri.'

'All right, Muniamma. Let my brother be a kateri. You do your work.'

'At least give some sesamem seeds and some raw bananas to a poor man of your caste on the thirteenth day. He can go in peace then. If you find it difficult to buy this, I will buy it and bring it for you.'

'Muniamma, if you wash the clothes as well as you talk about these things, everything will be cleaner.'

Today, Tuesday, was not the day for the grief-enquiring visits. But this amma's relations were as bad as amma herself. They thought that in the first ten days anything could be done. Not after early morning, before bath. Now amma had finished her bath.

Through the bars of the door, she saw a fat old man, with discoloured teeth, standing there, looking impatient, as he had rung the bell twice.

'Yaar, saar?'

'I'm Goutami's cousin brother. Is she there?' he replied, in an irritated way.

'Your name, saar?' asked Muniamma.

'Just call her. First open the door,' he told her.

But Muniamma had already gone.

'Someone is asking for you,' she said. 'He says he is your cousin brother.'

So one more repetition of Achyutan's last moments. Let me see who this is.

She went to the door. The silvery shining chair with the wheels was there before her. She rudely pushed it aside.

'Hello Goutu,' said a well-remembered voice.

But her heart did not leap with a remembered joy. It stayed in its place, calmly beating, her hand did not put itself out in a gesture of total contact.

She opened the door. 'Oh it's you,' she said.

It was Krishnanand.

So what do you think? I ask my granddaughters this question. Young ladies now, looking very beautiful.

'Your cousins are so boring ammamma,' says one.

'I think grief-enquiring visits are barbaric,' says the second, from a height, 'I think you should be allowed to feel sorrow in private.'

Private? But you do feel your sorrow only in private. Who can plumb the depths of that despair? Who knows the sadness of loss except one's self?

These children are too young. I am very old and uninteresting, their scorn is openly visible.

They both rise, they want to go, they have come only because their mothers have told them to pay a visit to ammamma and their chitti.

'Bye, ammamma, bye chitti,' they chorus. The silver chair's wheels have stopped, she is waving with a clumsy hand. Her expression does not change. She knows very well that their clocks are set to a different time. She is not resentful, merely observant.

But my dears, I can tell you though it is very many years since this happened, now I am over eighty but I can remember what I felt.

Let me tell you, it is very important that you should know so that you will realize what this kalachakra can do in the course of its turning, without any help from anyone. I opened the door and he looked at me in the way he had, though I had to peel many layers of the face, like you do with an onion, or with a bandage, unwind, or peel, to get at that old face, the heavy-lidded eyes, they were the only thing that proclaimed the old owner, the fine body had thickened, the curly hair had all but gone, it hung in small wisps at the outer edges of his head, encircling it like a torn, white crown. His smile displayed teeth discoloured by paaku, the beloved crutch of those who drink, do they think we can't get the smell?

He came in and I didn't do anything. I just led the way to our sitting room and sat there, he asked me what had happened and I just told him the details. I heard my own voice, flat, expressionless, bored.

Bored. In a few minutes, he rose to go, I had already bid goodbye to him, he had no use for me anymore. Whatever lessons I had to learn from this man's presence in my life, I had understood. That was all there was to it. There had been no love. That is a permanent feeling, and it has many ingredients, dears, just as you make payasam from many things.

It has respect, affection, generosity. It has loyalty and truth and support. Would I ever find it? I didn't know.

Now at this moment, this man could go. He had outlived his usefulness.

'Now that I know your house, I can come at anytime and also meet with SKS,' he said. 'It is a long time since I met SKS.'

I did not answer. Our ways had at last severed connection. Right or wrong, that is the way it was. I shut the door and turned my back. I think he stood there for sometime, watching.

The next time Krishna came calling, Seshadri was in the back garden, sitting under the tree of the sleepy face, which had leaves and flowers which withdrew into themselves when the sun, the harbinger of day and light, driving his chariot across the sky, gave a final whip to his white and orange steed and drove them over the horizon.

He was in his usual attire, a veshti doubled up to his knees, a banian, his poonool, his only concession to his antecedents, with the child, sitting in the silver chair with the wheels, next to him. His expression was one of a man who had come to a conclusion. He was not looking for anything. His search for truth, for that is what his search had been, not for him the trivial impermanences of life, had come to fruition.

Watching them both from the door, through the bars, Krishna hid a smile. SKS had not changed from the days in the hills, the same oily hair, much more luxuriant than his, peppered with white now, the same measured movements. Muniamma opened the door. Goutu was not to be seen, he went through the backdoor.

'Namaskaram' he said, surprising even himself. Must be all this living in Madras.

'Oh hello!' said Seshadri. 'Retired now?'

'Yes,' replied Krishna. 'Had to give the younger fellows a chance you know,' he said in that airy way, with a facetiousness that had always set Seshadri's teeth on edge. So he hasn't lost his ability to lie, thought Seshadri. But today Seshadri just smiled and continued talking to the child, introducing her to Krishna.

She held out her hand. Krishna took it and said something.

They then continued their conversation, with Krishna a mute spectator. Neither showed the least discomfiture at his presence. Krishna glanced surreptitiously at the backdoor. Would Goutu come and rescue him from this?

Ah, there she was! Should he go bounding over to her, or would she come in her own enthusiastic way of the past, with her words falling over each other, covering the silences with the cloak of embarrassed high-voltage conversation?

She just smiled at him. So he walked to her, and they both went inside, to the hall where they sat on two chairs.

'So you went to England. At last,' he said. 'How did you like it? Fun, wasn't it?'

Fun?

Perhaps, if you didn't think about the back-breaking work she had done in order to keep herself and Meera going, or you left out the anxieties about a child who had to be taught everything, or you didn't spend a lot of time wondering what went on behind that calm brow, that serene expression of loveliness. It had been fun to learn that she had been chasing a shadow, that within herself lay the strength to fight the ghosts of the past, that there was no one outside who could be her knight-errant. And it had been fun to earn money to spend as one pleased, without having to lie or cheat about what one had done with the ten rupees that one had been given a week ago.

'Yes', she replied. 'It was—fun.'

'Where did you live?' he asked.

She told him the name of the place. It evoked so many memories, many more even than the many places that had been her home in the last thirty-five years, all to do with her coming out of that tunnel of dependence, of living on the fringe, of grabbing and clawing at happiness, thinking that it was bound up in the person of someone other than herself. In this man sitting opposite her, waiting for his every whim and fancy, just because they had a shared past, something she had been denied with the others. She had had to live with the aunt of the diamond and silks, with her earrings shaking, sending out spurts of sparkle as she walked with that air of authority, her silk saris shining with a myriad colours, who now lay dying, sparkle and colour and memory gone, all that splendour leaking down the gutter of eternity.

Seshadri came in, slightly surprised to see them sitting in silence, generally Goutu had so much to say, especially to this fellow who, Seshadri had divined long ago, had been something more than a cousin to many of the girls in his family.

The child followed, none of her equanimity scattered, Seshadri went in to wash his hands.

'Why don't you to stay to tiffin?' was all he said.

Tiffin! Did they remember that disastrous day over forty years ago when he had been invited to tiffin in their home in the hills, when Sridevi had declined and he had gone, only to make a re-entry into Goutu's life? He looked at both of them from under the shade of his eyes. Seshadri was as controlled as ever, Goutu less so. She remembered, she looked at him and gave a smile.

As he ate the dosais, with their crisp golden shine, as he dipped his fingers into the sambhar, again his nostrils betrayed him. It was the old house by the Vaigai, the one where he had found most happiness.

It was she who brought it out in the open.

'Thinking of Thatha's house?' she asked. 'Does this make you think of Thatha's house?'

He half-smiled then, and said 'Yes'.

He didn't say any more and neither did she. Seshadri sat and ate with utmost concentration. He drew his chair back and the moment, with all its magic, passed.

He too got up, not quite sure of what he must say or do, next. She brought out the coffee, rich with the timbre of home-roasted and home-ground seeds. Seshadri had always been very fussy about details such as these. The colour was perfect, a brown of the deepest mahogany, the aroma gently wafting him to a place of happiness and peace. Sehsadri set down the tumbler in its davra and looked at him as if bidding him goodbye. He must go now, Goutu was not going to make it easy for him any more.

He left her house and walked towards the road where he might get a taxi. What had he seen there that was new? A new Goutu was what he had seen. Had she left it all behind her, were there not to be any more excursions into the past with her? He quickly caught this thought by its throat and put it to death: no, that was not possible. What would he do without this ally of his, this alter ego, who more than anyone else knew the demon of loneliness and non-acceptance?

Why had he played those games with her exuberance, her facility of meeting life with both arms extended, rushing to meet it according to her own terms, withholding nothing?

Had she become like everyone else now, studied with her responses, measured in her replies?

He had reached his house. The lighting, installed fifty years ago, was depressing. Ugly bulbs, resembling inelegant skulls, hung naked from their sockets. He looked at them, as if for the first time, the ceiling above the bulbs was darkened with years of neglect, as if reflecting the apathy of its owner.

He sat down on his unmade bed and wondered afresh about Goutu. Should he go back right now, this minute, and shake her by her shoulders, demand to know what she was thinking? Ridiculous he would look, Seshadri would think he had gone mad, but what would Goutu do? Would she smile at him in that new, maddening way, silent and controlled, or would he be able to re-establish contact?

She had been only too ready to tell him every thought flitting through her mind, butterflies they had been, going this way and that, settling on this detail and then moving on, excitedly turning from colour to colour, till his head had spun with confusion. He had listened with only half an ear, his mind occupied with other things, trivialities, thinking of her as unsophisticated, unlettered. He realized with a start that she was his closest companion, there was no one else who knew his backdrop the way she did.

No, he could not return now, he had to wait for a week at least, or he would look a fool in front of SKS and he also had to admit that he found Goutu's youngest daughter an embarrassment. The silver chair of the wheels, that stiff body, the speech so difficult to follow, at odd variance with her face, calm, unruffled, like a deep pool over which the wind may blow but which leaves no trace, they all combined to unnerve him.

He must have a bath, a bath was called for, the grief-enquiring visit was complete only after the first waters had been poured over ones head, but how wash away Achyut and those times they had spent together? Those movies, watching Laurel and Hardy or Charlie Chaplin, laughing in the dark, his fashionable, high bursts of laughter drowning out Achyut's self-conscious little snort, then emerging from the hall and making their way to the nearest coffee place, occasionally even a drink, just aiding life to become a little more mirthful, less trying, more easy to forget.

Good idea, the thought of a drink. He would have one now, his next step would become clearer. As he went to the rickety sideboard which served for what he grandly thought of as the bar but which looked as if it would crumble under his hand, his mind was a cauldron of regret. He stood looking down at the murky waters of the pool of his memory. Should he jump in? Or should he just stand at the edge, trying to make out shapes and then take wild jabs at what they might be? If he took the plunge, he might drown, he might never return from the water's depths, he might be swallowed by truth, that shark waiting to rip him from limb to limb in its attempt to get at his innermost core. No, he would not get in there, it could wait, this uncharacteristic desire to come to grips with himself.

The drink numbed his senses and amnesia, familiar and comfortable, went down to his very toes, stilling doubt and despair. No need for a bath now, after all a clean mind was more important than a cleansed body. That was the good thing about forgetfulness, there was no need to be troubled by these traitor thoughts anymore. He would go to sleep and there, in the tender arms of more forgetfulness, he would find rest.

He just lay down on his bed. Tomorrow would find its own way into the world. He did not have to help it arrive.

You know dears, it wasn't easy for me to turn my back on Krishna but it wasn't me who ignored him, it was another Goutu, a new Goutu. I can hear you asking who this is. I can tell you.

That Goutu—and I remember her well—still lived, but she was now in an inner room of this house of the self, I had understood her to be too precious to be shown to everybody, the Goutu of the truths which took birth in lies, who arrived at the same destination as everybody else but by another route, who had become battle-scarred, but through her own divinations.

I had not forgotten the thrill of Krishna's old beauty, the charm, the presence, the silences, studied and as powerful as his speech. No, as he sat with us eating that dosai, opposite my husband, who gave nothing away, my breast was surging with the weight of the past, the weight of abandonment, of non-belonging, of discovering the obvious.

The old Goutu, warring at this very moment with the new one, would have got into a rickshaw and, passing several traffic lights and turnings, come to that old house by the temple, the house with its paint peeling off, the small overgrown patch in front, unkempt with years of disuse with a fountain in the middle of it, and knocked on the door.

I want to talk to you, the old Goutu would have said, and she is within me still, she has not left, I have lots to tell you. Let me in.

What might he have done then? Would he have opened the door and given me that old half-smile, the one all of us, I, Kamakshi, Valli, Narayani, vied for?

Then?

In the old days, we had held hands, yes dears, I don't want to hide this from you, we had even kissed, and there had been a great exchange, from sadness to happiness, from loneliness to comfort, from standing there, outside the house to being brought in, from the white of the coldness of the aunt of the diamonds and silk to a room with the red and yellow walls of two people who found repose in this warm room.

Would we have sat there, my hands in his, drawing from each other the other's strength and demanding to be given the right to be us, he and I, I and he, all at the same time?

I don't know the answers.

What about this Goutu then, this new person who did not rush to meet the waves beating on the sands, who had merely smiled at Krishna, for once reading his mind like an open book, knowing that the experience of sitting at table with my husband, with his self-contained silences, made him talk more, as they made me say things which I did not understand or think about, speaking only to cover the quiet of facing the self?

We did not like the persons we were, Krishnan and I, we trembled with fear at the sight of that grotesque caricature, called ourselves, with our insecurities and fears out in the open, varnishing ourselves, covering with paint the real people we were.

And so we had gone on, saying something here, something there, touching this and touching that. We might have faltered and fallen without holding on to each other, who knows how?

I think of this now as I sit here and truth to tell, I can't really tell you any more about what might have happened. Krishnan is not here anymore, nor is my husband, of all of us only Uma and I are left. We do not speak to each other, she and I, haven't spoken for years. There is a great mist between us, I can remember how, in that country across the seas, there would be fog, great thick grey curtains of it, blotting out everything between the seer and the seen. Sometimes you could hear a voice or a car, but they would vanish past like ghosts. Uma is on the other side of this fog and sometimes I hear her voice, mingling with the voices of the others, over them all, the voice of their mother, my venerable aunt, whose ears would start to shake the minute she set eyes on me, radiating fire from the diamonds on them, fire would appear, too, from her eyes, and her voice would be red and scratchy from her hatred of me.

I remember the first time I told Krishna about this, the aunt's fiery hatred. He smiled and said that I would have to find my own comfort, and I did. I found him.

So why was I not looking at him now, seeing not the fat, thickened man, but the slim and tall manmathan of my girlhood?

Why was I not stretching across the years and seeing him?

No dears, there comes a time when no other person is needed to complete one's self and one's understanding. It was now Goutu, with all her loves and hates, her many little trips into make believe, who could staunch the flow and stop the waste.

So it was that I did not get into the rickshaw and run after him to explain or be understood. The time for that had passed. Now we had to gather ourselves into our own selves.

I wonder if he would understand.

Seshadri

That fell trickster, Time, had cunningly flown past and no one had noticed. In its wake, many changes had taken place, clever artist as he is, the changes were not even apparent till they had been wrought. A little white here and a little black there, a little slowness, sight and hearing were withdrawing into their seats, but no one ever knows when it happens.

It happens when we are not looking, thought Seshadri, and it seems we are never looking.

Now, at this moment, he looked at himself in the mirror, a very rare occurrence, the only other time being the daily shave, a man's way of navigating a razor on his face to face the rest of the day and the world, and did not count.

Standing there with the greatest concentration, he decided that the three lines of vibhuti, moistened with a drop of water in the palm of his hand and applied to his forehead, were parallel to each other and needed no further adjustment.

Having decided this he left the bathroom, yes, the only mirror in the house was the small one over the bathroom basin, Seshadri did not countenance anything more frivolous than that. Anything else was a waste and encouraged self-absorption.

He came out and put on his shirt, laid out for him by one of the girls, perhaps even one of his granddaughters. It was white, white being the only colour he ever wore. His veshti had two fingers of jarigai at the edge, he tried not to be too critical of this extravagance because it was a gift from his daughters. So was the shirt.

In the adjacent room, there was a flurry of activity. Goutu was putting on a new sari, araku with a border of manjal, a fiery combination which she had always liked. A lot of noise was emerging from the room, two daughters and their daughters were in attendance and the child was sitting in the chair of the wheels at the entrance.

Seshadri could hear every word.

'How do I look?' Goutu's excited voice came through and he could hear the girls' humouring comments.

'Lovely....' The rest was lost in the loud laughter that followed.

Seshadri sat in the hall, pretending to read the paper. Narcissistic, that is what she was. She would make them all late, with her genius for distraction.

One of the girls came out. It was his second daughter.

'Appa you look really handsome,' she simpered.

Seshadri made some noises, non-committal, he hoped. He had made up his mind to play along today, the girls and their husbands were taking a lot of trouble over this.

'Is your mother ready?' he asked, knowing what the answer would be. She would not be ready.

He suspected that there was a bottle of scent in the controversy–stirring bureau. She used it sometimes, he had caught a whiff of it, strange, unnatural, chemical, when she went out on one of her jaunts. He heard the bureau door being opened for the hundredth time that morning, the bureau was the repository of their mother's faith in them. It increased their solidarity with her, they knew, even if he didn't, the details of its contents.

The girls went back into the room with a cold cloth in which malli had been wrapped and stored last night in the fridge. This was for all of them to insert into their hair, this was a process and they liked to do it for each other. A small strand must be taken out, like this, held between the fingers and then the malli, doubled up would be put in, into the gap created. The hair style must not be disturbed.

The bureau was opened-for the last time?-and he knew the scissors were being replaced. This Seshadri approved of, that was one thing about her he had always liked, the order and the method in her housekeeping, at total variance with her thought process, which went by no rule book.

At last. They were coming out, one by one, led by the child, the chair of the wheels had been given a careful polish for this day.

Seshadri lowered his paper a fraction. He wondered how she looked in this particular sari, he had thought it a trifle garish, a sober grey would have been more becoming.

But she looked as she had always done, beautifully groomed, tidy, not a hair out of place.

The girls came out, the rani's attendants, and the granddaughters followed. He thought them very attractive girls but a bit too loud. Self-opinionated too. Pity his grandson was not here, but then he had gone away to study and Seshadri had absolutely vetoed the suggestion of his coming down by plane for one day. It was an excess he could not allow.

One of the sons-in-law brought out his camera, they all arranged themselves and their faces in the right way for a photo, with him and Goutu in the middle surrounded by the others. Seshadri smiled mentally, though he looked steadfastly at the camera, his expression serious.

This was his eightieth birthday. He was eighty today, the star of the day, mrigashirsham, had been on the ascendant on the day when he was born in his grandfather's house. His mother had been fourteen. A magnificent life had been foretold, a boy born under this star, proclaimed in the Gita by Sri Hari as being Himself, did not need further help. The time had come for him to move into sannayasa. He had seen the faces of his grandchildren and there was nothing more for him to do. It was not given to every man to witness a thousand moons in the company of his wife, to have a family which revered him. He thought he had detached himself well enough from the enticements of the world. Now he would give them up altogether

They were, for today, as Vishnu, the Indweller of all, and His consort Lakshmi, who, fickle as she was, had never left his side, or as Shiva, the ascetic who lived in the burning ghats but was steady in his love for the daughter of Daksha.

They got in the car and made their way to the hall where there was going to be a function for his long life and health, and since in his long life and good health lay the happiness and contentment of his wife, Goutu's prosperity.

Already the music of the nadaswaram filled the air, smells of incense and flowers assailed the nostrils, vying with the aroma of sambhar and rasam. The cooking had already begun.

He got out of the car, Goutu followed, she was smiling at everyone. Both sisters had come to attend this function, they had of course been present at his marriage to Goutu and he wondered what they remembered of it.

Did they remember the fifteen year old Goutu, sniffing and sulky, her uncle and aunt who had taken the place of her parents because her mother was dead not allowing her father to do kanyadaanam?

Did they recall her brother? That silent, unfriendly fellow?

He would not ask. It was improper to show that he was feeling nostalgic and sentimental.

The vadhyars started.

Shuklambharadaram vishnum chaturbhujam....

and

Gananam ganapathim havamahe......

and so on.

After the initial ceremonies were over, he and Goutu, sitting side by side, could go and sit on the chairs arranged in the hall. Everyone he knew, including Padmanabhan and his wife, yes it had been a friendship that spanned six decades, came up to him and Goutu. Lots of namaskarams followed, Goutu was in her element.

Then she spotted Krishnanand, she hoped he would have had the sense not to reek of liquor, and her mind went back, back, in the manner of a yogic posture, until it could reach back no more.

She saw in her feverish imagination that distant day—when was it?—when he had been sent down the stairs, not even to be a guest at her marriage.

The years had rolled by, who had pushed them? And here they were, more than half a century later, he was coming into this hall, towards them, Shiva and Parvati, or Vishnu and Lakshmi, have it how you will, they were a celestial couple for the day, having achieved mastery over their senses after a lifetime of grihastashrama, having faced and successfully conquered the many demons that frequent the path of householders, to try and test their devotion to the path of duty, singly and together.

She looked at Seshadri. Had he noticed Krishnanand, who had been waylaid by one of the others in his path?

Actually, Seshadri had. He did not think it necessary to register the fact. Krishnanand no longer had the power to distress him with his presence.

It was only Goutu who had this strength in her hands, with her vibrant presence which either banished or included people in her embrace.

He spotted the child in the distance, calm, collected, with no outward display of whatever she may have felt about her inabilities. She seemed not to mind, care even, about her apparent difference from everybody else.

Krishna had reached them. In a grand gesture, he did namaskaram to Seshadri, who was a little older than he, Krishna, was. The histrionics were not lost on Seshadri. It was part of their common background, Seshadri suddenly thought. Goutu and Krishnanand. They loved the stage, an audience, and their entire lives were devoted to the uncommon, the non-diurnal, the exaggerated.

Having made this discovery after a half century of search for a clue to their dissembling and falsehoods, Seshadri was startled at his own perspicacity. Why hadn't he thought of it before?

But—would life have been any easier for him if he had? No, not likely.

Just then his sisters came up, one of them had come from a distant northern city and had forgotten these customs, her quiet face betraying no emotion, just a plain, unvarnished acceptance of life and its many tricks. He looked at the other. She had been brought here by one of her grandsons, so much for that nearly-forgotten day when she had been accused of being barren.

Both his sisters had been widowed, he had gone when their husbands had died, for the tenth day ceremony in order to stand by his nephews as they collected their mother's thaalis in a bowl of milk, that thaali which had been tied with agni for a saakshi, was so full of the fire of their pativrata that it had to be put in a bowl of milk in order to cool its potent power.

No emotion had been displayed but when he returned, Goutu had been in a ferment of questions. Had they cried? Had the children been inconsolable? Had he felt grief at the passing of his brother-in-law?

Despite knowing her powers of dramatization, he had been angry. No-one he knew had ever been inconsolable. In his family, death was accepted as part of life. He told her so, flatly.

He did not say much to either, just some Tamil noises and contrasted this with the loud talk and excesses going on around him. Everybody was talking all at once, now Padmanabhan was saying something.

'You have beaten me to it' he was saying, 'my birthday of a thousand moons is two months from now. My sons will be here then.'

'Good, good,' said Seshadri. Something like a warm emotion passed in the look they gave each other, they had been two boys, both unlettered in the ways of city life, with all their worldly possessions in one tin trunk, firm in their purpose of leaving the mire of large families and poverty behind them. Neither had ever looked back, except to attend the death of their parents.

The vadhyar was signalling furiously, holding up a single finger, the sign to the nadaswaram players to rise to a crescendo. Seshadri went towards the fire, with Goutu following and there, amidst raining flowers and popping flashbulbs, tied a thaali round Goutu's neck, a thaali that had been encrusted with red stones and a diamond to show that the wearer had done enough punyams in both this life and in the previous ones to merit being the wife of a man who, in the course of a single human life, had seen the waxing and waning of a thousand moons.

As he tied the thaali, Seshadri's heart asserted itself and he felt a great longing for the days that had flashed past. What would he have done differently? He couldn't answer, because now they would have to adjourn for the feast.

Goutu, lying down on her cot after all the excitement was over and they had got home, went over the day's events in a daze. Where were all the intervening years? What had become of that girl, fiery, passionate, unmindful of consequence?

Where had she gone? Had the years eaten away at her? Today when Seshadri had tied the ruby-encrusted thaali round her neck, for a moment she had wanted to shout 'Stop! Stop!'

Why ?

Luckily, the impulse had passed almost as soon as it had risen.

What would have happened if she had?

What would everybody have done? She had wanted to say it on that distant day when the first thaali had been forced on her neck. She would not have dared to.

Why had she wanted to say it today, after all these years?

Then why didn't she?

Was it possible that after all these years she had understood the part Seshadri had played in her life? The steadiness, the decency, the loyalty, the unerring choice of what was right rather than what was easy, were these the reasons she had not said it?

She thought back on the many incidents, beginning with calling Krishnanand to tiffin because he was her cousin on that distant day a lifetime ago.

Then, the silence when her father had begged him to allow her, a thayilla child, to stay. He had been humiliated, but had he done the right thing?

And the child, had he put her first?

Then, coming to the hospital with her when Achyutan had died.

What about her? She thought him boring. But when she went down the wells of time, wherever she went, whichever path she had taken, he had been present, his eyes glinting behind the spectacles, his oiled hair drawn back from his forehead, she found that boring too, but his rectitude had given her a sense of the present, of the here and now.

She turned over and her thoughts turned to Krishnanand. He had been her past, that lonely faraway past where she had not counted in anyone's scheme of things. What part did it have in her life now?

This morning, in her new sari, she had felt some of that old excitement returning, that thrill of anticipation, which made everything appear new, gave even dullness a shiny edge. The guests had infused her with a new ardour, had given her the importance she craved, so that she had glittered like a piece of glass in the sunshine, or droplets of rain through which sunshine passes, filling them with rainbow hues

Her imagination had taken flight then, she was the chief guest, she would be gracious and charming. The newly found restraint fell away like an oversize coat, she would not today fit into the straitjacket of the behaviour expected from her.

She had had a few words with Krishna. She had been sitting on her own. Seshadri was talking to some friends.

'I didn't ever think that I would be present at this function,' he said, 'you did well Goutu.'

She looked up at him, unable to follow what he meant.

He answered her enquiring look.

'You did well by marrying SKS,' he said. 'He is a man I admire.'

Admire? She thought he had felt bored, this interesting man with his sense of humour and ability to make a joke of anything, turn any situation into an occasion for laughter.

She said so to him.

He looked at her, as if framing something he had in his mind, but he thought better of it.

'How do you feel?' he asked her, instead. 'I think you are only one of the girls to reach this exalted status,' he said, in that half-mocking way of his, which once had the power to send thrills though her body.

She ran her mental eye through the list of their cousins. Yes, he was right. She was the first one in that large assemblage of girls in that great house by the river Vaigai, the one that she did not quite belong to, in it but not of it, the others had become widowed or their husbands were younger than Seshadri.

How to answer this question? How did she actually feel? A sense of anti-climax hit her, she was close to tears.

He continued to look at her, realizing this and he said, 'Give me your hand.'

Was he mad? On her husband's eightieth birthday and she all of seventy and Krishna nearing eighty himself!

'Don't be silly', she replied.

She looked at him then, really looked, after many years and thought with a pang, he doesn't look well. Why is his face so yellow? And his eyes are dimmed with an odd dullness. What has he done to himself, this once -beautiful man, who we all loved so well, from whose lips the lightest utterance seemed like a pronouncement ?

A hundred questions sprang to her lips, about Sridevi, about his life in Jabalpur, about his drinking, about the women he was supposed to be friendly with. Out of this mélange of questions, bubbling inside her, she asked only one, something she had been curious about for years.

'I wrote you a letter once,' she said. 'Did you get it?'

'Yes,' he replied, 'Yes. I did.'

Suddenly it became important to know what might have been.

'Achyut told me he had ordered you to leave,' she said. 'But what did you come to do?'

'Nothing, Goutu,' he said. 'I came only to see you get married. Achyutan did right by sending me away. It was right for you to marry SKS. Achyut and I were alike, neither of us knew anything about marriage. Or about anything at all.'

So, she would have had this life anyway. She would have been Goutami Seshadri.

She looked away. She had been right. Some things could not be envisaged in any other way. Then how explain this feeling of sorrow, grief, even, that passed through her heart, piercing her through her body, squeezing some innermost place till the blood seemed to have drained?

She could not speak.

'I'm leaving,' he said and he held out his hand. She took it in both of hers.

A great surge of feeling went through her heart.

'I'll come and see you some time,' she said.

He held his hand for a second longer.

'Perhaps,' was all he said.

She watched him weaving through the crowds, going to Seshadri and saying something.

Seshadri actually put out his hand and shook Krishna's. Krishna smiled and he went off.

She watched him go.

She never saw him again.

This can't be true Goutu thought, as she put the phone down.

It was from Narayani, the excited relayer of death messages.

'Goutu, something bad has happened. It's Krishna. He died.'

Narayani didn't know what she was saying.

'What are you babbling?' Goutu asked.

'It's true. My servant's friend works in his house. There was a big crowd this morning it seems, as she went to work. When she went closer, she was told that her saar had died.'

'But how? When?' Goutu asked.

'Last night or this morning, I think. What a handsome boy he was. How we all doted on him!'

He was there just a week ago for my husband's birthday, how could he be gone? thought Goutami.

Goutu sat down on the chair closest to her. Meera came up to her, silent. Goutu took her hand. In the stiff fingers there was compassion and strength, in the calm expression there was total understanding.

'Krishna mama has died,' she whispered. Her voice seemed to be coming from a far distance.

Meera said nothing for a moment.

She found her voice. 'Everyone has to die,' she said.

Goutu looked at her. Meera was gathering her strength for her next pronouncement. Lips, tongue, throat, lungs had to be perfectly aligned for speech. Each of these Meera was bringing into her control.

'It's the natural end of life,' she said.

There, she had shown her mother her understanding, what lay behind the calmness, the control.

Did you not wonder, my mother? Did you not want to know who I really am?

I want to be more than what I am, what this chair of the wheels would proclaim me to be.

'What shall I do?' Goutu asked, stupidly, her thought being blinded by the abruptness of the parting.

'It will be all right, amma.' Again that air of the finality of one who has lived through several rounds of birth and death.

Seshadri walked in from somewhere, and even in her confusion, Goutu noted that his slippers were caked with mud, the floor would now have to cleaned again.

'Krishna mama has died,' said Meera.

Seshadri said nothing. Sitting in a room with two people of such superior understanding and acceptance, Goutu felt stifled. She had to settle her own mind, her heart must be stilled, her understanding, so lately and hard won, must assert itself. Discrimination must be used.

As she rose, she found, on trembling legs, she nearly stumbled and fell, so this was sorrow, dukham, she had not felt it for Achyut, nor her father, nor any of the other cousins.

But with Krishna gone, what would the world be like?

She tried to re-order the train of thought that was running feverishly through her head, what memory must she choose, before what? What came after that one?

Seshadri appeared in a veshti and shirt.

'I'm ready,' he announced.

Where was he off to? She looked at him, uncomprehendingly.

'Don't you want to go to his house?' he asked.

Munaimma was standing, watching.

'I'll be here', she said. 'You go'.

Goutu just stood there. Go to see that familiar face drawn in the stiffness of death? Or that wonderful body stilled forever?

And the voice? The voice which had had the power to wake her from the dead, now gone?

'I don't want to go,' she said. 'It's all right.'

'You'll feel sorry later, amma,' said Meera.

But how did she know this? Who had she seen die? Why was she, Goutu, feeling that, for the first time in her life, she was being guided to do the right thing, not having to find out for herself or being given orders?

Meera moved away. The chair of the wheels clanged as the wheels turned round and hit her bangle each time, had turned its back on her.

No, she decided. Whatever she might feel later, now she could not face it. She would not go. She told them so.

Seshadri made no answer. He put on his slippers and left the house. He would go.

When he returned, she looked at him. Were there any hints of what had happened on his face, his person? He went in for the customary bath, he would wash away, with the first waters he poured over his head and body, any traces of the memory of the person called Krishnanand, who had played such an important and long-lasting part in his life, spanning nearly six decades their uneasy relationship that had today come to a close.

He said nothing. Goutu would have to worm it out of him. What did she want to know anyway? How he had died? What had happened? What he had said? How he had been discovered?

Seshadri had taken her at her word. If she said she would not go, then the logical conclusion was that she did not care. She knew this. She would phone Narayani and find out.

At lunch, Meera asked.

There was a silence as she got ready to speak, preceded by a searching look she always gave before she spoke.

'What happened, Appa?'

'No one knows. The maid came and found him gone.'

Goutu had to be satisfied. No speculation was permitted. You either had the facts or you didn't. If you didn't, no guessing was allowed. There was no inane discussion on 'Do you think....?' Or 'I feel....'

All right, she would ask Narayani, she must wait till Seshadri went on his walk.

But Narayani beat her to it.

The phone shrilled its presence, Goutu, her nerves already taut with grief and frustration, nearly jumped out of her skin.

It was Narayani.

'What happened to you? Why weren't you there?'

'I had work. I couldn't come,' Goutu said.

'But your husband was there. You could have come with him.'

Even under the watchful eyes of Seshadri, Goutu decided to ask.

'What happened ? Do you know?'

'No one knows. They think it was his liver. Drinking so much wine is very bad for the health. He was always at the wine shop. You know the one near my house? My grandson used to see him nearly every day. He would come and tell me. I would feel so ashamed. Your cousin, Pati, my grandson would say....'

Goutu had to staunch the flow.

'When is the cremation?' she asked.

'Didn't your husband tell you? He was taken away by one of the children of ....'

Here she stopped. Goutu understood. His father's second wife, the one they didn't know, nor ever cared about.

She decided that she too would be philosophical.

'Written on his forehead,' she said. 'How can that be changed?'

There was some comfort in uttering these banalities, they lent reality to the situation.

Narayani made some clucking sounds, signifying total accord.

'Seri, then,' she said. 'Come over some time. I think very few of us are left. Let us meet.'

Goutu put the phone down. Yes, they must meet. Soon the entire clan would have gone, the younger members of the family didn't even know each other.

For the hundredth time, she felt that her life lay bound up in the life of her family, a family she didn't know, never had.

The rest of the day passed off, she made a mental note of the date. All those years of longing, of the closest she had come to love, of desire, had found their end on this date.

Her first home, the strange meeting outside a shop on the Mall, the many secret visits he had made, rendering her life so far from her desultory home bearable, even his absence from her wedding, more significant than his presence might have been, their parting, his sudden re-entry, his presence in this city of their retirement—all of it must mark this day as their end.

Had he tried to tell her something on that birthday? Now even the birthday had taken on a new significance as the last time she had, unbeknownst to her, met him.

Why hadn't she given him her hand when he had asked for it? What was convention if it tore you from what you wanted most to do?

And why had she ever thought that she no longer had any use for him, that he had become unimportant? She had thought herself to be stronger than she was.

She put her face on her pillow. Sleep at last blanketed her and muffled out the sounds in her head, the unending train of thought and memory that she was being cut asunder with. Let it go, her mind was saying. It will not come back again.

Meera

And so it was that at last I became an important member of the family, one who had shown an understanding of the idea of death which agreed with my father's understanding of it.

Krishna mama's passing away had been the end of many things for my mother, and ushered in her own ending as it were, it was clear that we were all entering another period, one that must be used for untying the knots of the heart, which hold us prisoner of our own lives.

I don't think I can tell you how exactly the next few years slipped away, but the signs were all there, the signs of dissolution which precedes creation, but which is not understood as such. My sisters, unhappy at the way their complacence was being threatened, and being beset with their own troubles, shouted angrily at the slightest hint of change.

I watched them both in their descent from life, slower and slower their hearts beat and they became more and more uncaring. Nothing mattered much, not even visitors who they had once cherished.

There is no exact moment when all these things happen, so no one knows when you can no longer do this or that. But because I knew about being unable to do what one wants to do, I felt the difference.

I had learnt a lot about not being able to move this limb or that one, of not uttering this sound or that. I also knew that if I couldn't do these things, people thought my mind and its understanding were absent.It was perfectly clear to me that in this world of strictures, being different is the one thing that people fear greatly.

I watched the day passing into night before my very eyes, but unlike those who are afraid of the dark, I knew that the sun would rise again. I watched my father and mother take longer and longer to do things, but I took so long that it did not seem a particularly sad thing. I saw their minds closing as flowers do when the sun is setting, my mother's zest for the new slipping until it almost disappeared from view. My father, calm and undisturbed, remained the same. Life's little turns and twists were not beyond his understanding.

All this I saw with my inner mind which is as good as anyone else's but is not recognized as such.

Then one day it happened that my father died. But know that I remained unafraid. It was the others who thought that death is a final parting.

Goutu

Goutu looked at Seshadri.

He had become more scholarly, he was always reading and he had certainly changed since the passing of Krishnanand. He sometimes read things aloud to Goutu, who found that she could not always understand what he said.

Five years had passed since the birthday of the thousand moons but age had not diminished his buddhi, though it had increased her fears. She felt afraid of anything that didn't fall within her comprehension.

The children visiting her had ceased to signify, nothing mattered any more. She found, however she scraped at her memory, she could recall very little of the house by the river Vaigai, she sometimes spoke with Narayani, whose grandson had broken her heart by going away to America. With no further need to make tiffin, Narayani was useless.

Their lives were now very simple, proceeding on a straight and narrow path, no little journeys to explore the new. Seshadri often thought that, yes, he would not be afraid when the end came. He had lived long enough, had, he thought been successful, but he had not been able to receive Goutu's love, nor had been able to conquer his desire for it.

He had done his best. A man could do no more than what he had done. At every juncture—and there had been many such—he had thought of the greatest good. Let things happen as they must, he could not change anything. He felt death approaching on certain days, he knew that his heart was telling him something important and he had understood its message.

He felt feverish, he must ask the doctor though he felt it was not necessary, the girls insisted and he must do their bidding, not appear to be in an unseemly haste to depart. He came back with a packet of pills but his vision had dimmed and he knew that he was reaching the end of the journey.

Goutu too knew that this man who she had journeyed with on life's path, with all its many unexpected turns, would drop off from that path before too long and she would have to continue on her own, with the child. There was no place for fear in her heart, it had ceased to be the place where she processed her thoughts.

He now owned, as in his student days and even the days before that, only two veshtis and shirts. It was a deliberate attempt to cast off the unnecessary details and items of life. He wore clothes to protect himself from the elements and to observe the basic tenets of human decency. He had an umbrella and a cloth bag which took the place of the briefcase he carried when he was working.

He thought he had taken sannyasa as he had wanted to, on his eightieth birthday, and he had stilled the fires in his heart and mind and no longer had any desire even to acquire knowledge. His memory, as acute as ever before, played no tricks with him. He recalled his grandfather's Upanishadic pronouncements about vidya, knowledge, being relevant only if it were knowledge of the Brahman. The rest was all information.

His only weakness remained his desire to get Goutu's unqualified love but he knew that the time for that had passed. He had been ambushed there by the presence of Krishnanand.

And it happened that one night he was suddenly woken by a feeling of not being able to draw breath and found he could not even call out, he knew that perhaps it was all over, but whatever jolts his body took in the pangs that human beings feel when they leave this world, the death pangs as it were, as a fitting tribute to their mothers' birth pangs, no one would ever chronicle. He did not live to describe them.

So when Goutu rose the next morning and found that he had not got up at his usual hour, she went into his room fully knowing what to expect. But being in the presence of a force that controls life, and time, she shouted out, finding her breath coming in gasps, not being able to hold the phone or summon her daughters, someone had to do that for her.

They all came in various cars, the house was crowded with people, some crying, his sister telling her something, she knew not what, then her cousins, two of them.

One of the sons-in-law officiated. She handed him the darba grass, authorising him to act on her behalf.

Then they took him away, tied and bound so that he would not fall out of the van, for the last journey, this man who had come a long distance from the dark village, married her, slept with her, produced children, traversed the distance with her.

Later that afternoon they returned, her son-in-law looking frantic with tension. Poor boy. She took his hands in hers and held them to her head. 'Thank you', she whispered.

Now she was in it, alone.

All right dears, so I am now without even that faithful man, my husband. Sitting here as I am doing now, with just the child, with all my life locked up in a box. Sometimes I open the great chest and take one memory or another out, and look at it and put it back. One thing I will tell you all and that is—it is difficult to know which is more important—the past, or the present? Or the future.

I now think that the past is the only thing we can be certain about because it actually happened and the present and future become the past without any trouble, even as I speak to you.

We spend our time together and as I sit with her hand in mine, I wonder what she will do without me. I thought that she would be the one I would always have with me, and I was not wrong. I also know what that beautiful face conceals, I have understood the secret behind the calm unruffled brow. It is the knowledge of the secrets of life and death. Why did I think she was burdened with no knowledge of speech or walking as I understood them?

So it was to understand this—real knowledge—that she was sent.

Long conversations we had, she and I, about those years that we spent together in the country over the seas, those walks, the snow, the people. Neither of us could believe that we had actually lived there.

My girls would come and go, their children had long since left their homes, so their houses, too, were as empty as this one was. I would look at them, bewildered and anxious they were, but I could not offer them comfort.

Only the other day, I had a strange dream. I went down a road—where was that road? In that country across the seas or was it up in the highest mountains? Or perhaps in some other place?

Wherever it was, I went down and I came to a few steps, and I went down the steps to see a dark room. I heard voices, yes dears, I could swear I recognized the voices, it was thrilling, there was Valli's voice, loudest of all.

'Let me in, Valli, it's me, Goutu'.

The door opened a crack and yes, it was Valli. She was wearing a pavadai and shokka. What? She was a grandmother. A grandmother with a pavadai?

But no, she was slim and her hair was plaited as we all did all those years ago and she had flowers arranged in that lovely dark plait.

'I can't let you in Goutu,' she said.

What! Was I to be banished even from here? Would I never have a place with them?

Behind her stood another shape. Tall it was and the set of the shoulders could only belong to one person. What were they doing here? Alone?

No they were not alone because in the distance I could see a young man, his face earnest and serious, thick black hair combed back, glasses glinting gravely.

Where was this room? Why was the beautiful koodam of the house by the river with its grandeur and grace and large space inside my house on the hills?

'I can't let you in. If you come in, you can't go back,' said Valli.

'I don't want to go back,' I cried. 'Let me in'.

'No.' She slammed the door shut.

I could hear myself sobbing, gasps, loud and hard, my shoulders were heaving, as they did when the aunt of the diamonds and silks denied my presence.

I thought I heard my daughters, why were they calling me and from where?

No, I would rather be with Valli and Krishna and wear a pavadai, have my hair plaited.

So I went back.

Dharmakka!

I screamed with excitement. There she was, that loving smile. The only person who cared about what happened to me.

Akka, I'm so glad to see you! I want to tell you something. Krishna said....

Dharmakka is looking worried.

I won't tell you. You'll tell Periamma and that will be that.

Dharmakka is looking away. No don't turn away Akka. Look at me.

She turns around. She is smiling. Don't tell me Goutu.

What! Dharmakka doesn't want to know? Then I will, must, tell her.

If you want to know... I begin.

No, she says, Don't tell me. Keep it to yourself.

She is joking. I laugh with joy.

I will tell you. You have to listen, you have to.

'Seri, shollu,' she says, relenting. What is it?

It's Krishnanand. We love each other. He wants to marry me.

Did he tell you that? She asks, her voice is a whisper.

No, but he said that I must go to Madras, I must stay with him. What does that mean?

Dharmakka turns away. I rush behind her, my pavadai flying in the breeze, my plait shaking from side to side.

The door opens. I follow Dharmakka, but she is nowhere to be seen. A huge rush of air coming from somewhere, my body? I am not sure, carries me along There is darkness, darkness, I fall into a deep well and am carried through the abyss.

'I'm sorry,' says the doctor. 'She has gone you know. She must have just slipped away.'

He folds his stethoscope. He puts it into his bag. The girls are looking at him, their mother has died and this man is carefully undoing his bag and putting away his stethoscope.

'If you send someone to the clinic, I will sign a death certificate.'

So in the next days, all the beauty, the contradictions, the talents, the sway she had held over them, the body which had faithfully done its best in carrying them, the fingers of the hands of that body, the fingers which had done diverse things, cleaning the utensils, enchanted them with the music they could coax out of that violin, the tongue that could speak in many ways, were all consigned to the flames.

The great light, the size of a thumb, which is lit when the life is made, had escaped through one of the orifices, and joined the elements, earth, water, air, fire and ether.

All that remained was a small mud pot.

As they had been taught by this woman, the girls did not bemoan the absence of a brother in their lives. Having consigned her to the purificatory flames themselves, they marched single file to the sea that laces the eastern side of the city and there, entering waist deep into the rushing waters, they set the pot down.

The waters of the sea, white and foaming, rushed towards it. Nothing could escape the waters, they would sweep away anything that came in their way.

It was carried away.

The girls watched the lonely pot being dragged into the depths.

They stood there for a minute, too numb even to weep.

Then they went back into the world, to live their lives made poorer by the absence of this one human being from whose bowels they had sprung.

Two or three gulls swooped across the sky, in wide and graceful arcs, calling to each other, as if welcoming Goutu in their midst.

The girls turned away, satisfied. She would not be alone.

As they turned, they saw, flashing in the last rays of the sun, the silver of the chair with wheels. It moved rhythmically as the wheels were turned, traversing some distance before they caught up with it.

No, she would not be alone. Her journey had only just begun.